JOE COL

Between worrying about my missing foster daughter, Emily, and trying to keep my wits about me in the face of danger, I don't remember the last time I've had a decent night's sleep. And don't get me started about the rift that gets wider each day between me and my wife. But it looks like I'm not the only one who is in dire straits. My honorary son, Sheik Ali El-Etra, seems to be in way over his head. He's heir to the throne and under pressure by his family to choose a bride. He's finally gotten serious about someone...but it's the last woman on earth I would have expected. Just between you and me, Ali thinks he's God's gift to women. And his feisty computer consultant-turned-girlfriend, Faith Martin, is hardly the type to bend to a man's will. Those two are like oil and water! Perhaps my troubles with Meredith have made me a cynic....Who knows, maybe Ali's bachelor days *are* finally numbered.

I Married a Sheik

Sharon De Vita

Silhouette Books

Published by Silhouette Books

America's Publisher of Contemporary Romance

Special thanks and acknowledgment are given to Sharon De Vita for her contribution to THE COLTONS series.

SILHOUETTE BOOKS
300 East 42nd St.,
New York, N. Y. 10017

ISBN 0-373-38706-7

I MARRIED A SHEIK

Visit Silhouette at www.eHarlequin.com

Printed in U.S.A.

THE **COLTONS**

Meet the Coltons—
a California dynasty with a legacy of privilege and power.

Ali El-Etra: *The powerful sheik.* Accustomed to having his minions scurry to do his bidding, this sultan is shocked—and infinitely intrigued—by his new consultant's irreverence. Has he just met his match?

Faith Martin: *The plain Jane.* Wary of high-handed "princely" types like Ali, she'd like to take the sheik down a notch or two—and then keep him in her loving arms forever!

Meredith Colton: *The misplaced matriarch.* With no memory of her true identity, the real "Meredith" has been having recurrent dreams about a little redheaded girl crying out for her help—a child that she instinctively knows is her own daughter!

Emily Blair: *A woman in jeopardy.* With little cash and a heart full of fear, the Coltons' foster daughter hitches a ride to Wyoming when she suspects she is the target in a botched murder attempt.

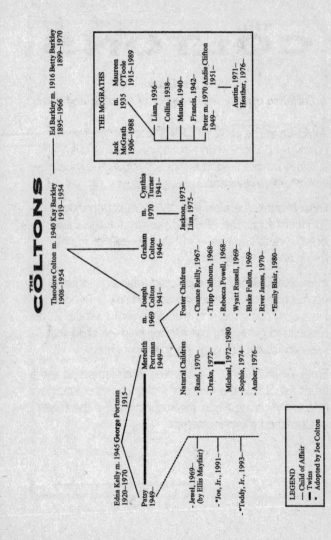

THE COLTONS

Theodore Colton m. 1940 Kay Barkley
1908–1954   1919–1954

Ed Barkley m. 1916 Betty Barkley
1895–1966   1899–1970

THE McGRATHS

Jack McGrath m. 1935 Maureen O'Toole
1906–1988   1915–1989

- Liam, 1936–
- Collin, 1938–
- Maude, 1940–
- Francis, 1942–
- Peter m. 1970 Andie Clifton
  1949–   1951–
  - Austin, 1971–
  - Heather, 1976–

Joseph Colton m. 1969
1941–

Graham Colton m. 1970 Cynthia Turner
1946–   1941–

- Jackson, 1973–
- Liza, 1975–

Edna Kelly m. 1945 George Portman
1920–1970   1915–

Meredith Portman
1949–

Patsy
1949–

Foster Children

- Chance Reilly, 1967–
- Tripp Calhoun, 1968–
- Rebecca Powell, 1968–
- Wyatt Russell, 1969–
- Blake Fallon, 1969–
- River James, 1970–
- *Emily Blair, 1980–

Natural Children

- Rand, 1970–
- Drake, 1972–
- Michael, 1972–1980
- Sophie, 1974–
- Amber, 1976–

- Jewel, 1969– (by Ellis Mayfair)
- *Joe, Jr., 1991–
- **Teddy, Jr., 1993–

LEGEND
- - - Child of Affair
▮ Twins
* Adopted by Joe Colton

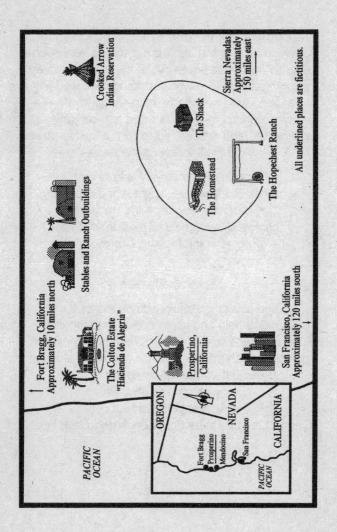

PACIFIC OCEAN

Fort Bragg, California
Approximately 10 miles north

The Colton Estate
"Hacienda de Alegria"

Stables and Ranch Outbuildings

Prosperino,
California

San Francisco, California
Approximately 120 miles south

Crooked Arrow
Indian Reservation

The Shack

The Homestead

The Hopechest Ranch

Sierra Nevadas
Approximately
150 miles east →

All underlined places are fictitious.

OREGON

NEVADA

CALIFORNIA

Fort Bragg
Prosperino
Mendocino
San Francisco

PACIFIC OCEAN

I suppose a woman who writes romances should believe in love at first sight, but it took a very special man to make a believer out of me. As I was deep in preparations for my oldest daughter's wedding, a kind, loving, wonderful man—a widower— walked into my life, uninvited and certainly unexpected, and proceeded to turn it upside down. And I will forever be grateful!

This one's for that very special man, who has brought love, laughter, and especially joy back into my life—and my heart. Thank you, sweetheart. This one's for you! —Colonel Frank Noland Cushing (Ret)

Acknowledgment

The author gratefully acknowledges the technical help and assistance of the following computer wizards who answered numerous questions with infinite patience and never laughed at this self-confessed computer moron! Any errors are my own. My heartfelt thanks to: Dennis Liby, Gay Wescott, Jason Arden, Dave Pede.

One

San Diego

Faith Martin was fuming.

Ignoring Mr. Kadid, the dark, elderly male assistant who had been keeping her company for the past hour and a half, Faith expelled an exasperated breath, side-stepped the man and made a beeline for the closed double mahogany doors.

"Wait. Miss Martin, you—you can't go in there." The words came out of his mouth on a near gasp. He was right on her heels, clucking his tongue in dismay.

But it was too late. Unwilling to be denied, she threw open the double doors and came to a stunned halt, staring at the unbelievable opulence.

"Good Lord." The words slipped from her mouth as her gaze quickly traveled around the elaborate of-

fice suite. She'd been in a lot of offices since she'd
started her own computer consulting business seven
years ago, many belonging to some of the wealthiest
entrepreneurs in California, but nothing had ever
compared to the decadent luxury of this one.

The enormous suite was breathtaking.

Done in subtle, masculine shades of navy and ma-
roon, the room contained a collection of exquisite art
she had no doubt was genuine. The walls were papered in elegant white silk with hand-carved mahogany chair and ceiling moldings.

In the middle of the room, backlit by a wall of
floor-to-ceiling windows overlooking the sprawling
city, was a large elegant cherry desk that looked hand-
crafted. In front of the desk sat two overstuffed navy
leather club chairs, each with its own matching ottoman.

On the walls hundreds of books were shelved,
some of which appeared to be rare first editions, giving the room a homey, comfortable feeling. In the
farthest corner of the room, in front of another row
of floor-to-ceiling windows, sat a long carved conference table with matching navy leather armchairs. A
soaring marble fireplace with an intricate coat of arms
above the mantel was nestled in another corner.

Placed around the room was an assortment of Wa-
terford vases displaying floral sprays in an array of
beautiful fall colors, permeating the room with a
sweet, almost sinful aroma.

The late afternoon sun danced through the windows, shimmering off the beautiful pieces and height-
ening their beauty.

Faith shifted her gaze. In the middle of this opulence, behind the desk, sat a large dark-haired man engrossed in a telephone conversation, totally oblivious to her.

He didn't even bother to glance up.

"Mr. El-Etra," she said, storming across the plush navy-blue carpeting to plant her tennis shoes squarely in front of his desk. "Mr. El-Etra," she repeated, more firmly this time. She was close enough now to see the family crest of gold inlaid in the top of the magnificent desk. It was a remarkable piece of work and almost had her gaping again at such decadent extravagance.

The man's custom-tailored suit in a subtle gray pinstripe probably cost more than her annual rent. If you added the custom-tailored monogrammed white shirt, it could probably cover her grocery budget for a time as well.

Terrific, she thought sourly, letting her gaze slip around the room again.

Annoyingly rude, unbelievably rich, and no doubt irresponsibly spoiled. Her three least favorite things about a man, let alone a client.

She planted her hands on his desk. "Mr. El-Etra, I appreciate that your investment firm is an important and integral part of the business community. However, you need to understand that my time is no less important or valuable." Faith paused to take a breath, vividly aware that the dark-haired man was not in the least bit aware of her.

Or her tirade.

He was so engrossed in his telephone conversation, she could have been an ant on the floor for all the attention he'd given her.

However, the rather nervous assistant now hovering at her elbow seemed about to swallow his tongue—if the bulging of his eyes and the nervous tic in his cheek were any indication.

Faith took a step closer to the gleaming cherry desk, her temper inching upward by the second as she glared at the man. It wasn't enough that he had kept her waiting for almost two hours, now he had the audacity to ignore her!

"Mr. El-Etra!" She rapped on his desk with her knuckles. He never even flinched. "Your managing director called me this morning and insisted I come immediately, that your computer problems were of an urgent nature, but it certainly can't be that urgent if you've kept me cooling my heels in your waiting room for almost an hour and a half."

"Uh…Miss Martin…" The assistant held a finger in the air. "It's—it's not *Mr.* El-Etra," he corrected softly.

Faith blinked at him and felt a momentary skitter of alarm. Good Lord, had she stormed into the wrong office? She almost groaned. That would be a perfect end to a perfectly dreadful day.

She took a careful breath. "Excuse me?"

"It's *Sheik* El-Etra."

Her eyes narrowed. "You've wasted almost two hours of my valuable time and now you're going to get picky about titles?" Her voice rose as she took a step closer to him, forcing him to take a self-protective step back.

In addition to cooling her heels in the outer office, she'd missed lunch and had sat for nearly two hours in rush-hour traffic in order to keep this blasted appointment.

She'd been unusually nervous and excited when she'd received the call, well aware of the prominence of the El-Etra Investment Firm, and what having its name on her client list could do for her successful, but still not-over-the-hump computer consulting business.

Nerves, however, had finally given way to an inexplicable bout of temper. She was successful, in demand, and had garnered an impeccable reputation in the business community and was not accustomed to being treated like a bad-tempered stepchild.

"Ms. Martin." The assistant's lashes fluttered nervously. "I'm certain—"

"No, Mr. Kadid, *I'm* certain that your boss's title is of the utmost importance to you." Planting her hands on her slender jean-clad hips, she turned to glare at the man still engrossed in his telephone conversation. "But trust me on this, I couldn't care less what you call him, although I'm quite certain I could come up with a few names on my own." She gave her head an arrogant toss.

"Now, if you'll excuse me, I really don't have time for this nonsense. Give my regrets to the sheik," she snapped, deliberately giving his title a great deal more emphasis than necessary as she turned and marched toward the doors. "Tell him when he gets serious about his business to give me a call. Until then, don't bother wasting my time." Muttering under her breath, Faith stormed back toward the still-open double doors, muttering imprecations under her breath.

"Miss Martin." The very deep, slightly accented

voice caught Faith off guard, stopping her in her tracks. She hesitated for a moment as that voice seemed to reverberate along her nerve endings like an unwelcome caress. A shiver raced over her and she turned on her heel in curiosity to stare at the man that voice belonged to.

He'd hung up the phone, and was now standing, drawn to his full, elegant height, and Faith resisted the urge to take a step back. She had to tilt her head to take in the full length of him.

Magnetic was the first and only word that came to mind, crowding everything else out. With his proud, regal bearing, and dark good looks, his presence was forceful, incredibly masculine and magnetic.

Magnificent was the second word that popped into her mind. He was, she decided, one incredibly magnificent-looking male.

At the moment, however, he was also apparently annoyed, judging from the stormy look in those dark, smoldering eyes. Her chin rose a notch.

Too bad.

So was she.

Unwilling to be intimidated by his looks or his posture, Faith took a step closer.

She'd been too irritated to pay much attention to his features before, but now she could see he was, in a word, incredible. Much more elegant and handsome than in the silly society photos where he was usually photographed with some bubbling, beautiful airhead clinging to his arm like sticky flypaper.

Burnished olive skin, deeply etched features, a thin, elegant mouth, large dark eyes and a head of thick black hair made him like look a renegade pirate from another age. An unconscious shiver raced over her as she felt the full force of that masculine pull.

That was until she reminded herself of his reputation as a playboy who went through women faster than a termite through rotted wood. She pretty much knew this was *not* a man she was going to have much in common with.

He reminded her too much of her father. Another handsome, irresponsible playboy who'd cared little for those who'd cared for him, less for the broken hearts he left behind.

Faith almost shivered. She'd made it a practice to steer clear of this type of man. Thank God she didn't have to deal with him on a personal level. She didn't have much patience for immature male nonsense, and what little she'd had her father had worn out years ago.

Having to deal with this man professionally was going to be more than enough, judging from this first encounter.

"Ms. Martin." There was a hint of annoyance in his tone and Faith took a step closer, wondering what the heck he had to be annoyed about.

"I believe we have an appointment?" One dark brow lifted in an imperious manner, only further annoying her. Impenetrable dark eyes stared levelly at her, as if taking her measure.

"*Had*," she corrected, marching back toward him, feeling as if his twin nearly black eyes could see through her. "*Had* an appointment, Mr....Sheik El-Etra." She tapped the face of her no-nonsense sports watch. It matched the rest of her no-nonsense outfit. "Almost two hours ago."

"It's Ali," he said quietly.

Faith blinked again, trying to shake off the shivers that deeply masculine voice had caused. It was an exotic blend, deep, smooth, with just a hint of an accent. "Excuse me?"

"It's Ali." He tilted his head, and she thought she saw a small smile curve the corner of that elegantly sculptured mouth. "My name, it is Ali."

His smile bloomed, transforming his face into something breathtaking. Faith felt her own breath wither in her throat. Her heartbeat sped up, and she resisted the urge to take a self-protective step back, to put some distance between them.

"Although I'm sure you've thought of other things you'd like to call me." Amused, his dark eyes twinkled, and Faith flushed, embarrassed that she'd allowed her temper to overrule her professionalism, and embarrassed that she was allowing herself to have such a strong physical reaction to him.

Her flush deepened. "I'm not accustomed to being kept waiting," she said defensively, meeting his gaze. "My time is at a premium—"

"As is all of ours," he countered, looking at her curiously. He was not accustomed to having a woman look at him as if he'd just slithered from between a crack in the flooring, and he was absolutely certain he didn't care for that cold look of suspicion she was aiming at him, as if she'd examined and found him lacking.

It was most unusual, and hardly the reaction most women had to him.

He spread his hands in supplication. "I apologize, but this delay could not be helped. I have been dealing with just one of many crises today. We will, of course, compensate you for your time, Ms. Martin.''

"It's not merely a question of money," Faith snapped, irritated that he apparently thought money was her only concern. "Some things are more important than money."

One brow lifted again. "Really?"

It figured he would think money was the only important thing. Something else he had in common with her father. Looking at him, looking into those dark eyes, she had the strangest feeling he was mocking her. Faith stiffened.

"To some people money isn't the be all and end all. It's a question of time and priorities. I have other clients who were in dire straits today and needed my assistance, clients I put off because your needs seemed to have been the most urgent. Apparently that's not the case."

"On the contrary, Ms. Martin. My needs are most urgent." The tone of his voice had changed, softened, making her think of other needs, more primal needs, and she felt an unfamiliar heat flare through her.

"And contrary to your initial statement, Ms. Martin, I take my business very, very seriously."

Fascinated, Ali studied her. She was, he decided, too plain to be considered beautiful, but there was something about her, even in her drab clothing, that was elementally interesting.

The khaki slacks fit snugly at her waist and flared over hips that were elegantly curved in a way that would keep a man's head turning.

The plain cotton T-shirt was baggy, yet didn't hide

the lush curve of her breasts or her slender, almost elegant shoulders.

Her hair, although pulled tightly from her face and left to hang down her back in some intricate braid, was a beautiful honeyed-auburn with every color of red woven in. He'd bet his next foal it was all natural, and complemented her ivory complexion in an extremely appealing way.

Her face was an interesting, feminine mix of angles with enormous green eyes, high cheekbones and full lips that were made for kissing and kissing well. Although judging by the looks of her, she probably hadn't been kissed very often.

She was not generally the type of woman a man pursued or fantasized over. She was far too plain. Her face was devoid of any cosmetics, yet her lashes were dark, long and full, shadowing her eyes and giving her a rather exotic look.

Ali found himself curiously intrigued and could not imagine why.

He gave a quiet sigh. Perhaps he'd been working too hard. An extremely sensuous man by nature who found everything about a woman, from her looks, to her scent, to the gentlest curve of her hip, gloriously fascinating and arousing, he had perhaps been too busy fending off the females his parents kept foisting on him to seek out a woman that could truly please and appreciate the most sensuous part of his nature.

Although he wanted—desired—the company of an intelligent female companion, one who was more than an advertisement for the latest designer, and who could respond honestly to his passionate nature, he had no wish or desire for love. It was simply not something he would ever allow in his life again.

Most of the women in his universe were either perfect models or beautiful debutantes who wouldn't dare go anywhere without being decked out in their finest designer apparel.

Their facades of beauty, minds of cobwebs and hearts of stone, which allowed little for true passion of any kind, had left him cold.

And a cold woman was the curse of a man's life. A fate worse than death, he believed.

In his experience a woman who was so preoccupied with how she looked rarely took the time to examine what she could feel, and a woman who could not accept, enjoy and appreciate the feelings of passion a woman was capable of was truly not a woman.

Ali cocked his head to examine the woman before him more closely, feeling a heated arousal of interest just from the angry passion radiating from her.

This was clearly a woman who allowed herself to feel all of life's emotions.

And he found her both interesting and intriguing.

It was just a shame she was so sullen and surly.

He was not accustomed to having anyone, let alone a woman, speak to him in such a disdainful manner. Women generally were falling all over themselves in an effort to impress him.

It had become truly annoying, simply because he didn't want to be impressed by beauty or clothing or jewels; he wanted a woman to impress him with her essence, her honesty, her being.

And so far, he had not yet met such a woman.

"Ms. Martin, if these computer problems are not

solved, and solved quickly, it will jeopardize the entire operation of El-Etra Investments, something I cannot allow. I have a responsibility to my clients. They have entrusted me with their funds, some with their life savings, and I don't intend to cause a panic among my investors because of a silly problem with a machine.''

"Silly problem with a machine," Faith echoed in disbelief, blowing out a soft breath. "Mr. El-Etra, if it wasn't for that silly machine, I sincerely doubt you'd be in business. That machine has no doubt improved your productivity and saved time, not to mention money.''

"Are you scolding me, Ms. Martin?"

His words hung in the air for a moment, still soft, still polite, but with an underlying hint of power. Faith had a flash of awareness that perhaps she'd gone too far, but she wasn't about to back down. To anyone.

"Just stating facts, Mr. El-Etra," she replied coolly. She refused to use his first name or his title, which would put this situation on a more personal level and she intended to keep this strictly business. "So exactly what is the problem?" she asked, determined to get on with the business at hand.

He smiled. "If I knew, Ms. Martin, trust me, I would have fixed it myself, or had my staff of computer experts attend to it. I'm afraid that we are at a complete loss to understand this confounded system."

She tried to place the accent, but couldn't. There were definitely hints of English, probably Oxford, she surmised, but there was also a hint of whatever his native language was still detectable in his impeccable speech patterns. It was an enticing blend of something foreign, exotic and slightly…erotic.

He dragged a hand through his dark hair. "All I know is that this problem has disrupted my entire operation, and it simply cannot go on or be tolerated. I must have the problem fixed immediately."

"Immediately," she repeated with an irritated nod of her head. Obviously this was a man who was accustomed to getting what he wanted when he wanted it. Spoiled, she thought again, realizing she'd been right about him.

Her eyes flashed. "Well, if I hadn't been cooling my heels in your waiting room, perhaps I'd have a clue what the problem is and be well on my way to solving it."

"Perhaps." Apparently, she was not about to forgive him so easily. "I understand that you are considered the best computer consultant in the business?"

"Considered?" One auburn brow rose and Faith felt the stung of his subtle doubt. Fists clenched in frustration at his high-handed arrogance, she took a step closer to his desk. "Well, you've apparently been misinformed."

It was his turn to look surprised. His glance shifted from her to his elderly assistant who was still quietly hovering in the background. "Kadid? What is this?" He glanced at Faith, his dark brows drawn together, then back at his assistant. "Have I been misinformed?"

The carefully chosen words sounded like a threat, almost making Faith shiver. The guy gave a whole new meaning to the word *arrogant*.

"Absolutely," Faith responded before the assistant could. "I *am* the best computer consultant in the business."

"Modest, too, I can see," Ali said, with a cautious smile of relief. Plain, but feisty, he decided with a hint of amusement. An interesting combination.

"No, Mr. El-Etra, not modest, just honest." Her chin lifted. "Honest, and the best, but my time is valuable, and I don't appreciate having it wasted."

There was anger, he noted, and something else radiating from her, something he couldn't quite place.

"Nor do I, Ms. Martin," he said, making it clear that he considered her little temper tantrum a waste of his time. "If you are the best, then I trust you'll be able to fix this insidious problem. Immediately." It was a clear challenge, one Faith couldn't ignore.

"Well, I don't know about your idea of immediate, but once I find out what the problem is, I'm sure I can fix it. I can't tell you how long it will take, though, until I know exactly what we're dealing with." She met his gaze head-on. "Some things take time whether we like it or not." And she was not about to be rushed. Sensing he was going to issue another order or command that would no doubt only tick her off more, she rushed on. "Now, if you can give me an idea of just what the problem is, it might help. I have to start somewhere. I'm good, but I'm not a mind reader."

His gaze lingered on her a moment longer, stung once again by her sarcasm. He drew himself upward, slipping his hands in the pockets of his pants. "We are a full-scale investment firm, Ms. Martin, and once a month an assortment of checks are issued to each and every client, checks of different denominations for different purposes, of course."

"Of course." She wished he'd stop staring at her. He was making her…itchy.

Ali blew out an exasperated breath. "A few days ago, on the first of the month, when the first batch of checks were distributed, the system began spitting out checks in the wrong denominations. In addition, we discovered that it was also crediting deposits to the wrong accounts and in the wrong amounts. Both new funds, interest, as well as divestitures were misappropriated to the wrong accounts."

With a shake of his head, Ali glanced down at the neat sheaf of papers on his desk. He'd spent hours going over paperwork, trying to fix this problem, then more hours on the phone, soothing investors. He felt as if he hadn't left his office in weeks.

"As a result, chaos has reigned. My accountants did not discover the errors until after the first checks had been mailed and the first irate calls started coming in." His brows drew together as he remembered the flurried panic among his staff that morning.

"Our in-house computer experts were at a loss as well. They began searching for the problem—"

"Immediately," she injected with a nod of her head, causing him to stop and stare at her for a long moment. Obviously this was a man not used to being interrupted, judging from the look on his face.

"Yes," he said slowly, still watching her carefully. "But alas, they came up empty. They tried various things, unfortunately, nothing worked. As a result, we had to completely shut down our entire computer system simply because it is set up to distribute and print checks automatically. I have been deluged with calls from angry investors who have either not received the proper funds or have not received any funds at all. Now, unfortunately, they have begun to question the integrity as well as the security of my firm." He sounded as if he was surprised by this.

"Well, that would do it for me." She slipped her hands in the pockets of her jeans and rocked back on her heels. "If I'd invested my life savings in a firm and found out they'd screwed up and sent my money to someone else, I'd be a tad annoyed as well."

"Screwed up?" His dark eyes narrowed and she could hear Mr. Kadid sigh from behind her. Apparently telling the sheik he'd screwed up wasn't part of the proper protocol. "This cannot continue, Ms. Martin," he said in clipped tones. "So as you can see, this *is* of an urgent nature and must be attended to. Immediately."

Perhaps if he hadn't sounded like he was issuing a command, she might have softened at his plight.

"Situations happen whether we allow them or not. And as for urgent and immediate, I'm not the fire department," she clarified, watching his face darken. The assistant was apparently back to sighing again as well. "Clearly you've got a problem with your accounting program," she said, meeting his gaze. "But it wouldn't take a genius to figure that out."

He stiffened and his eyes went cold at the perceived insult. "I can assure you, Ms. Martin, that my staff is more than qualified to handle almost any situation that arises—"

"But apparently not this one. If they were, I wouldn't be here."

Her words hung in the air for a long moment, and Faith wondered if perhaps she'd gone too far. But the man was just so…downright arrogant, she couldn't help but goad him a bit.

"Touché." He nodded, as if he was gracing her with some great gift, and allowed a small smile to touch his lips. "But of course you are right. This was one problem my own people have not been able to solve." He paused for a moment before continuing. "El-Etra Investments prides itself on its impeccable reputation. As I'm sure you can understand, when someone trusts you with their money, any hint of impropriety can have devastating effects, not just on your actual business, but also on your reputation. And in this business, your reputation is everything." He took a slow, deep breath. His gaze never left hers. "I have assured my investors that this problem would be solved immediately, and although I have ample insurance to cover such an occurrence, it is my name on the firm, and I have vowed to personally make good on every single penny invested and due. We're in the process of personally distributing checks now to every investor to cover any losses, differences or discrepancies. "

"You have that kind of money?" The question popped out before she could stop it. She glanced around. This was no mom-and-pop store, but a big-league operation that no doubt had millions of dollars invested in it.

The mere idea of having that kind of indeterminable wealth almost stopped her heart.

For someone who had struggled, pinched pennies, worked two jobs just to put herself through school, and had gone deeply in debt just to start her own fledging computer consulting business and had worked like a dog for seven years to make a go of it, the thought of endless funds seemed like nirvana.

And this man discussed it without so much as a blip in his voice.

"But of course," he said simply, as if they were talking about pocket change. "Why, are you planning on raising your rates?"

She couldn't help but grin. "Well, I hadn't thought of it before, but now, I just might consider it."

"Ms. Martin, I *am* Sheik Ali El-Etra." The way he said it made her wonder if she was supposed to bow or something.

"So I've heard, since everyone around here keeps telling me, although I can't possibly imagine why." Apparently she was supposed to be impressed.

She wasn't.

"It means nothing to you?" For a moment he didn't know if he should be annoyed or amused. Most women he encountered had all but done a Dunn and Bradstreet check on him before he ever met them.

"I don't have a clue what your title means or why it should be important to anyone but you."

He couldn't help the little stab to his ego. "My title, Ms. Martin, merely means that I am of royal blood."

"Royal blood?" One brow rose suspiciously. "Right." This time the sigh from behind her was louder, and laced with just a bit of…panic, she thought. "Royal blood?" she repeated with a frown, considering. "You mean like a king or queen or something."

"Or something," he admitted with a slow nod.

"And of course no one thought it was important to mention this little tidbit to me?" she asked, feeling just a tad embarrassed by her own behavior. He *was* a client, and just because he'd been rude, didn't mean she had to be.

He just annoyed her so with his arrogant, high-handed orders and demands. As if the world revolved around him.

"Would it have changed your behavior if you had known?" Or your viperous tongue, he wondered.

"Probably not," she admitted honestly. "Unless you have the power to have someone beheaded."

He threw back his head and laughed, the sound rich as it rumbled around the room. "I'm afraid, Ms. Martin, that we no longer behead people." He flashed her a brilliant smile. Faith felt as if the temperature in the office rose twenty degrees. "Too messy."

"Well, I'm grateful for small favors."

Cocking his head, he studied her. "And would it have mattered anyway?"

"The beheading?"

He shook his head, amused. "No, my bloodlines."

"Not unless you plan on running in the Kentucky Derby." She shrugged. "Otherwise, your bloodlines don't matter one whit to me."

He laughed again. It had been a very long time since anyone had dared to speak to him so freely. Not since his beloved grandmother. But this woman certainly did *not* remind him of his grandmother.

On the contrary, she was young and vibrant, with a sharp mind and an even sharper tongue. And he found himself suddenly both irritated and amused by her.

A woman who was not impressed by his title, his bloodlines or apparently his money. A novelty, for sure.

"My title, it is, as you said, perhaps, of no real importance," he admitted, "except to those who are impressed by such things." He smiled and she realized anew just how incredibly attractive he was. "And you apparently are not one of those people."

She shrugged. "I couldn't care less if you're the King of Siam."

"Wrong country, wrong continent." He pointed to a large, full-scale color map framed and anchored to one wall. "The land of my birth is Kuwait, Ms. Martin. "

Faith glanced across the room to where he was pointing. The details of the map were so precise, so vivid, it actually looked hand-painted. Probably was, she decided. He probably had his minions paint the little trinket just to decorate his office. Why, she wondered, did the mere thought annoy her?

Faith shifted her gaze back to his. Kuwait. So that explained the faint accent, the inlaid family crest on his desk, above the fireplace. It explained a lot of things about him.

She'd been right; he was spoiled and rich and, on top of it, a royal. Terrific.

"You are frowning again, Ms. Martin. Have I said something to annoy you?" Apparently, he'd been saying and doing a lot that annoyed her.

"You can call me Faith," she said absently. If the man had royal blood, she supposed he could use her first name. "So what is a man of royal blood from Kuwait doing in California?"

"What all normal men do, I suppose. Conducting business." He cast another scathing look at the computer on his desk. "Or trying to." He didn't know why it was important to explain, but for some reason he did. "Many years ago my father and his partner, Joe Colton, who happens to live in Prosperino, California, went into business together. It was the perfect merger of two like-minded men, two countries and cultures."

"I've heard of the Coltons," she said with a quiet nod.

The Coltons were California's version of royalty—well-connected, well-respected, and with a sterling reputation in the business, political and social community.

She'd always admired the vast family from afar, eagerly reading about them in the paper, envying them for their closeness, their love, their incredible devotion to one another. The Coltons were, in her mind, what the definition of what a true family was, the kind she'd never had.

But her affection for the Coltons went far deeper than what she'd read in the society pages. The Coltons were a philanthropic family, giving to a great deal of needy causes. They had, in fact, funded the Hopechest Ranch, where she'd spent some of her teen years. Without the ranch, she would have probably ended up on the streets, just another lost kid.

She owed a lot to the Hopechest Ranch and, ultimately, the Coltons for making such a place possible for children who either had nowhere to go or had no one who wanted them.

She'd been just such a child. But she wasn't about to tell this man any such thing. Someone like Ali El-Etra would never understand what it was like to be alone in the world, never knowing where your next meal was coming from, never knowing if you'd have a roof over your head.

He had minions who did nothing but hand-paint maps for him. Obviously he'd never understand where she came from.

Ali continued. "My father is a descendant of the Kuwaiti royal family, and our family is the largest land-holder in our country, land that is rich with oil. Oil my country was not even aware of so many years ago, nor did they have any experience extracting that oil from the land. Joe Colton, on the other hand, had equipment, experience and an oil-rigging company." Ali shrugged, not mentioning how close the El-Etras and the Coltons had become over the years. They'd been like a surrogate family to him, particularly during the years of unrest in his country, when his father, fearing for his safety, had sent him to America, to the Coltons, to live.

It was a painful time for Ali, a time when he'd been separated from his family, and when he'd lost his beloved Jalila.

Ali shook away the memories, preferring not to think of them. They were still far too painful.

"Together, Joe Colton and my father became not just partners and very close friends, but very, very successful men." He shrugged, his massive shoulders moving beneath the custom-tailored suit. "It has worked out quite well for all concerned."

Faith glanced around at the room. "Apparently," she said with a nod and a smile. Her initial assessment of him had been accurate. He was an impossibly spoiled man who had no idea what it meant to work. A man who'd been handed everything in life. A man she could never relate to or understand.

She was proud of all that she'd worked for and accomplished on her own, without any help from anyone.

But then again there'd never been anyone to help her, she thought. She had no choice but to do everything on her own.

She shifted her gaze back to him. "So it's daddy's money you're pledging to cover your investors." She nodded thoughtfully, trying not to feel envious. "Now I understand." Cocking her head, she met his gaze. "I imagine it's easy playing at being successful when someone else is footing the bills."

"My father's money?" The words boomed out of his mouth. His face darkened, and an unrecognizable emotion swept through his eyes as he shot to his feet like a cannon.

"On the contrary, Ms. Martin. It is *my* money," he corrected firmly, coming around the desk to stand in front of her. He was so close she caught a hint of his aftershave. It was something discreet, masculine, and absolutely intoxicating.

At a distance, he was impressive; standing so close, his presence was nearly overwhelming. She could see the tiny pinpoints of annoyance glinting from his dark eyes, eyes that were nearly hypnotizing. She could see the way his mouth tightened, thinned.

"Ms. Martin, I came to America and started El-Etra Investments on my own nearly ten years ago, without any assistance from my father or my family, financial or otherwise." Feeling defensive, Ali glanced around the spacious room. "The only assistance my father has provided to me has been advice and counsel, something I value tremendously since he is not only successful, but a man of quality and integrity."

He paused to level her with a gaze that almost had her quaking in her shoes. "My father was one of my very first clients, but make no mistake, Ms. Martin, my father is not a fool. He would never have entrusted or invested part of the family fortune in this firm if it was not a viable business enterprise."

Faith watched him warily, the way she would eye a hungry rabid dog she'd suddenly stumbled upon.

Apparently she'd hit a nerve, one that was particularly sensitive. He was fairly quaking with anger, and his dark, fathomless eyes were hot enough to singe the hair on her head.

Apparently she'd really put her foot in her mouth this time.

Faith wanted to sigh as regret swept over her. She realized she needed to pull back, get some distance, emotionally and physically, and apologize.

She didn't want to do anything to jeopardize this job. Not because he was of royal blood, or rich. Neither meant a hill of beans to her.

But his business did.

She needed it in order to secure the bank loan that

would help her expand into larger offices and hire a few more consultants. But none of that was possible if she ticked off El-Etra and lost this account.

In spite of her own apparent disdain for the man and his lifestyle, she needed to remain emotionally uninvolved, not let her own personal feelings about his life, his reputation or his wealth affect her business sense.

Detached. Completely and totally detached. She had to remember that. Looking at him, she had a sinking feeling it was going to be easier said than done because he represented all the things she detested in a man.

"I'm sorry," she said quietly, vividly aware that he was still standing just a few inches from her, far too close for comfort. Close enough for his male scent to tantalize and tease her senses. Close enough for her to see how attractive he really was. It was totally unnerving. "I didn't mean to insult you or your family."

"Family is a very sacred thing to me, Ms. Martin," he said quietly, sincerely. Still, it sounded like a warning.

"I'll try to remember that," Faith said with a nod.

"Please do." His eyes had cleared and his face had softened into a small smile. The man was far too gorgeous to be allowed to smile in public.

He looked at her carefully, as if studying her. "It would be a pity if I had to reconsider my position on beheading, don't you think?"

Two

"The thing I don't understand, Ali, is how you've managed to stay in business this long?" Shaking her head, Faith took a sip of her soft drink and glanced across the conference table at him.

She'd been working on his systems nearly round-the-clock for the past three days, trying to navigate her way through the problems.

Lack of sleep, lack of food, and a headache had left her hot, tired and more than slightly irritable, but patience wasn't her strong suit even on her best day.

She hoped this meeting didn't take too long. The man still made her nervous, with his dark good looks and his impossible smile. Several times during the past few days she'd found her thoughts drifting back to their initial meeting.

The fact that she also found herself scouring the

society pages each morning to see if his picture was there—invariably it was, with a different beautiful woman each day—had become a mild irritant, something she didn't understand.

She was not the type of woman to spend her time mooning over a man. But she consoled herself with the thought that it was only natural for her to be curious about a man who held her financial future in his hands.

The pictures each morning only confirmed and emphasized their differences and her rather jaded opinion of him.

He apparently had a different date every night. She couldn't remember the last time she'd had a date. By choice. She much preferred machines to men—machines didn't lie, they didn't leave you and they couldn't hurt you.

"What do you mean?" he asked with a frown.

Faith sighed, realizing she'd been staring at him. The sun coming through the windows glinted against his facial features, highlighting the plane of his cheeks, the curve of his jaw, already dark with an early afternoon stubble. The total effect was irresistibly sexy. No wonder women swooned at his feet, obeyed his every command and begged to do his bidding.

Annoyed by her own train of thought, Faith shook her head, averted her gaze, then glanced back down at her notes, trying to get her mind back on business.

"Okay, Ali, let me explain what I've discovered so far." She struggled to concentrate, took a breath so her voice would be calm. "First and foremost you need a new server. The one you have is not only hopelessly outdated, but not nearly adequate for your needs. I'm surprised you haven't had a serious problem before this.'' Carelessly, she flipped through her notes with a frown, then glanced up at him, surprised to find him watching her intently.

The way the man focused his total attention on you made you feel as if you were the only person in the world. It was unnerving, and a bit annoying.

She wasn't accustomed to being scrutinized so closely by a male, particularly such a potent male. It was definitely having an effect on her, and only increasing her nervousness and irritability.

''Second, you need a completely new operating system, something you'll be able to use not just today, but in the future as well. In addition, each workstation needs new, updated monitors, keyboards and programs that will complement the new operating system.'' She stopped, rubbed the throbbing in her forehead, then sighed, wishing she could read her own handwriting.

''And above all, Ali, you have to install anti-virus programs on each and every workstation. With the proliferation of viruses out there, you're far too vulnerable without it. I think that's what happened to your system. I think you picked up a virus somewhere, probably in an e-mail attachment from someone, the kind that sics itself onto your hard drive, and then begins eating your files.'' She sipped her warm soft drink, wishing for a hot sandwich and a colder drink.

She shrugged her slender shoulders. ''That's the only thing I can figure out right now. It's the only explanation I can find. I've checked and rechecked everything else.'' And she had the headache to prove it.

He leaned forward in his chair, his concentration total. ''Do you mean that perhaps someone has done this deliberately?'' Concern etched his words and she sought to soothe his worry.

''Deliberately?'' She considered. ''No. Not necessarily. Certain software is particularly vulnerable to this type of virus. Hackers think it's cute to send viruses out that disrupt businesses and destroy data.''

''This type of thing is done for fun?'' He looked so shocked, she laughed.

''Believe it or not, yes.'' She cocked her head. ''Guess you're not in Kansas anymore.'' At his frown, she realized he didn't have a clue what she was referring to. She laughed. ''Never mind, it's just an expression.''

''An expression?'' He continued to frown. ''What does Kansas have to do with my computer system in California?''

Amused, Faith realized she was going to have to give him a crash-course in American pop culture. ''Did you ever see the movie *The Wizard of Oz?*''

He looked both suspicious and skeptical. ''No. Should I?''

''Yeah.'' She smiled and leaned her arms on the table. ''It's a great flick. Anyway, 'you're not in Kansas anymore' is merely an expression, a takeoff on the movie's theme. It just means someone's being particularly naive about something.''

''And am I being naive?'' he asked carefully, wondering if she was once again making fun of him.

Uh-oh, she had a feeling she was about to put her foot in her mouth again.

She chose her words carefully, not wanting to insult him further. She rather liked having her head where it sat.

"Ali, I know it's hard to believe, but some people do deliberately try to disrupt businesses and destroy data merely for their own pleasure."

"That is a very sad state of affairs."

"I agree."

"But because of them, you have a job, correct? Then perhaps you should show some appreciation?" The amusement glinting in his eyes made her realize that he was teasing her. It took her by surprise.

"You've got a point there," she admitted with a smile.

"But if you think or even suspect this was deliberately done to disrupt my business, I shall need to get my security people on it."

The way he said it made her think he was about ready to call out the royal national guard.

"Now wait a minute, Ali, don't get your shorts in a crimp. I don't think this was deliberate. I think someone was just careless." She held up her hand before he could speak. "Not necessarily one of your employees." She didn't even want to go there, fearing his reaction. She certainly didn't want to be the cause of someone losing his job. "Sometimes you pick up a virus and you don't even realize it until your system is affected. So for the time being, I think you'll need to be very, very careful. I'd instruct all of your employees not to open any e-mails from anyone who is not known to them."

"Okay." He nodded slowly as if deep in thought. "I shall have Kadid attend to it immediately."

"Good." At least the man was taking her advice, something she was certain he had difficulty doing normally. She wasn't certain if it was because she was a woman, or simply because he was a royal. In either case, she had a feeling Ali was more accustomed to issuing orders than to taking them.

"Now, once I install the anti-virus software, it will run automatically every time the system is booted up, and every time one of the workstations is turned on. It's not foolproof, but about as close as you can get. Once that's done, about once a month, you should have your systems people do a sweep for viruses of the entire system. Do you understand what I'm saying, Ali?" He looked blank as a blackboard.

Ali shook his dark head, his eyes bemused. "Viruses. Servers. Systems. Boots." He held up a hand. "I do not understand all this technical jargon." He watched her, entranced by the intensity in her vivid green eyes.

Faith was a woman, he'd discovered in the past few days, who appeared to be passionate about everything. There was so much about her that was different from the women in his life. She was proving to be a refreshing change. And a challenge.

With her back against the windows, sun spilled into the room and over her, glinting off her hair, making the reddish gold strands shimmer like spun gold.

He found himself wondering if her hair was as soft, as silky as it looked. He laced his hands together on the table to prevent himself from finding out.

Today, she was once again dressed in her beloved T-shirt, well-worn jeans and tennis shoes.

Instead of a braid, though, her hair was caught up atop her head in a knot, but some tendrils had escaped and now framed her face in a riot of red and gold. She had the most incredible skin, like the tip of a rose before the first bloom.

He sighed, trying to get his thoughts under control. "You will have to explain what I need to do in a language I can understand. Preferably English or Arabic."

"Arabic's definitely out," she admitted with a shake of her head. "I'll stick with English. In layman's terms your system is having a…" She searched for a term he could understand. "A techie tirade."

His brows slowly drew together over confused dark eyes. "A tirade?"

She nodded. "You know, a temper tantrum." She smothered a chuckle at the look on his face. Obviously no one had ever thrown a tantrum on the sheik before. Well, there was a first time for everything. Faith sought to soothe him, instinctively reaching out to pat his hand. "But you don't have to worry about it, Ali, or understand it. That's what you're paying me to do."

And paying her well, she thought. His offer of a very generous bonus if she could get his new system up and operational within ten days was a challenge she simply couldn't resist. It might prevent her from having to go to the bank, hat in hand, and beg for another operating loan.

The bonus would go a long way toward giving her the financial cushion she hadn't hoped to have for at least another year. And when she added her regular fees on top of that, she'd be able to not only expand her offices and hire two consultants, but she might even be able to swing some new equipment as well.

The promise of the financial windfall had caused her to bury herself in her work, barely leaving this building except to stagger home for a few hours of sleep. All in all this was turning out to be a dream job.

Now all she had to do was control her mouth and her temper, not to mention her inbred annoyance at what this man represented to her.

She probably should have considered a gag, Faith realized. It might have been easier. .

Ali sighed. "I don't know how much longer my staff can continue to work the enormous hours necessary to do everything by hand." To say nothing of the hours he'd spent on the phone trying to soothe clients. "Can you complete all this in a week?"

"Once I go over all the financial concerns and get your permission to order the necessary equipment, I should have you up and operating at full speed in *less* than a week." That was with her working nearly round the clock, but she was counting on that bonus. She frowned thoughtfully. "I've been testing the system this morning, so it's up right now, but I don't suggest you use it for anything important, at least not until all the new equipment is ordered and installed."

Ali nodded, listening to her. He shifted his weight, then loosened his tie. In spite of the fact that it was late September, someone had apparently forgotten to tell Mother Nature, for the temperatures were still hovering near the 90s. In spite of the excellent air-conditioning system, it was getting warmer by the minute in his office.

"It's not necessary to go over the finances, Faith." He waved away her concern. "Purchase anything you need. Kadid will take care of all the necessary paperwork." Ali got up, went to his desk and pressed the intercom. "Kadid, could you come in please?"

Faith had learned that the elderly assistant had been with Ali since his birth. She and Kadid had become fast friends.

In the past few days, she'd found Kadid to be helpful and cooperative, not to mention exceedingly kind and totally devoted to Ali, which, she had to admit, she found surprising.

Kadid readily kept her supplied with cold colas during the day while she worked; something she considered fuel to keep her going. And she praised him regularly for it.

Yesterday, Kadid had even sat for a moment and shared a cola with her, no doubt breaking some sort of royal protocol.

A moment later the double doors opened and Kadid came in. "Ms. Martin." Smiling, he gave a slight bow in a way she found totally charming.

While Ali dressed in Western business clothing, Kadid dressed in traditional garb. Flowing cotton pants, shirt, loose moccasin-type shoes, and a long, almost floor-length sleeveless robe all in a sedate shade of beige.

She smiled in genuine warmth. "Hello, Kadid."

"Kadid, Faith will be purchasing some computer equipment for the company. Please see to it that she has the clearance to spend whatever amount necessary.''

Kadid nodded. ''Of course,'' he said, turning to Faith with another smile. ''I shall take care of it immediately, Ms. Martin.'' In spite of her insistence that he call her Faith, he retained his thoroughly formal manner.

Looking hesitant, Kadid took a step closer to Ali to speak privately. ''I beg your pardon, Sheik El-Etra, but Mrs. Jourdan's in the waiting room. She does not have an appointment, but she is…concerned about a matter and asked if she could wait to see you.''

''Maureen is here?'' Ali frowned, then walked around to the front of his desk. ''Please show her in.'' He turned to Faith. ''You do not mind? This should only take a moment. Maureen is a very old and very dear friend, not to mention a client.'' He straightened his tie, smoothed down his collar. ''If she's upset I need to see her.''

''Not at all.'' Faith leaned back in her chair, oddly surprised that a man like Ali would take the time to personally soothe the concerns of one client. She would think he'd leave the day-to-day business to his staff.

''Show her in immediately, Kadid.''

A few moments later, Kadid led a woman of about seventy into the room. Smartly dressed, she wore a sapphire-blue suit that seemed to match her eyes, and carried a wolf's-head cane that she leaned on heavily. Her shock of silver hair was cropped close, but elegantly styled.

''Maureen.'' With a look of pure adoration that transformed his arrogant face into something almost breathtaking, Ali went to her, took her free hand in his and kissed it gallantly, making the woman smile. "It is good to see you." He kissed her hand again, and Faith could see the genuine affection radiating from him. Curious, she couldn't help but watch. "It's been too long."

"It's good to see you, too, Ali." She kissed his cheek in return. "And you're as much of a charming rascal as ever," she said, giving his hand an affectionate squeeze.

"I saw your parents at Joe Colton's birthday party last night. It was good to see them again." The woman's brows drew into a frown. "You heard about the attempt on Joe's life?"

Ali nodded. "Yes, I did. I spoke with my father late last night and he told me about it." The attempt on Joe Colton's life, in his own home, at his own birthday party was simply beyond comprehension.

"I can't possibly imagine why anyone would want to hurt Joe Colton."

"Neither can I," Ali concurred with a nod. "But I'm afraid there are some very sick, irrational people in this world." Ali shrugged. "I'm certain the police are doing everything they can to find the culprit."

"Mmm…I hope so." The woman glanced around, then spotted Faith. One elegant brow lifted as she turned back to Ali with a mischievous smile. "Well, well, well, I'd say your parents' taste in women is finally improving."

He laughed. "No, Maureen. You misunderstand." He glanced at Faith. Their eyes met, held, and Faith felt a sting of heat arc and sizzle between them. Stunned, she tried to shift her gaze, but found she couldn't. It was as if his magnetism had taken hold of her and refused to let go.

There was warmth and humor in his eyes that softened his arrogant facade and almost took her breath away. He seemed much more human this way—and so much more dangerously attractive.

"Maureen, this is Faith Martin, a computer consultant I've hired to handle this ridiculous problem we're having."

Maureen looked at Faith again, then sighed. "Pity. She's lovely."

"Yes, I agree." As Ali glanced at Faith again, their eyes met, clashed, clung, and she flushed, stunned by his comment and the look in his eyes.

She was entirely certain no man had ever called her lovely before. Nor could she recall a man looking at her quite the way Ali had just looked at her. It made her skin flush, and her heart skip a beat.

Still smiling he turned back to the older woman. "So tell me, to what do I owe the great pleasure of your company? It's been too long, you know. You promised to have dinner with me last month." Ali held her hand as she lowered herself into the club chair, setting her cane next to her. Ali sat on the ottoman in front of her, giving her his full attention.

"I'm fine, Ali, truly." She sighed and adjusted herself more comfortably in the chair. "I know I promised to have dinner with you, but I don't like to leave Alfred alone in the evenings if I can help it." She smiled up at him. "You know how much he enjoys company." She reached out and took Ali's hand, holding it like a lifeline. "The staff told me you stopped to play bridge with him one afternoon last week.''

''And he beat me soundly.'' Ali's eyes twinkled. ''But please do not let it get around that I was playing hooky.'' He leaned close and dropped his voice to a scandalous whisper. ''I was supposed to be at an investors' meeting. If Kadid finds out I was playing hooky, heads will roll.''

''You devil.'' She laughed, giving his hand another affectionate squeeze.

''So what brings you here?'' There was concern on his face, in his eyes as he watched her. ''You know all you have to do is call and I will come to you.'' She looked so troubled, he laid a hand to her cheek. ''Maureen, tell me, what is it that is troubling you?''

''You always could read me.'' Her smile was tremulous. ''Ali, I've brought something for you to look at.'' With a frown, she dug an envelope out of her black leather handbag. ''I received this notice from the rehabilitation center.'' Ali took the envelope, removed the contents, then began reading.

''They're raising their rates again, I'm afraid.'' There was a small catch in her voice. ''I thought I'd better bring it to you to look at.'' She watched him as he read. ''I'm very concerned. You know, Alfred has been doing so much better there. It's the first place where he's actually shown some improvement.'' She bit her lower lip, a sheen of tears in her eyes. ''I really don't want to have to move him, but I'm not certain I can afford to keep him there if they keep raising their rates. This is the second year in a row. I don't know how much longer—''

''Maureen.'' After folding the letter back in the

envelope, Ali took both of her hands in his, kissing the fingertips. "I have told you before, do not concern yourself with these financial problems. Your investments are all solid and secure, and growing day by day. You have entrusted me with these financial matters and I would never let you down. I take my responsibilities seriously."

She scooted forward. "Oh, Ali, I know, I wasn't questioning—"

"Yes, I know, Maureen." Patting her hand, he smiled at her. "You have more than enough to worry about now, and as I've said in the past, there is more than enough money to take care of whatever needs you or Alfred have now or in the future."

Some of the worry left her face. "And you're sure, Ali? I mean, I know how expensive all of Alfred's care is—"

He touched her cheek again. "Please, Maureen. Trust me."

"Oh Ali, you know I trust you. Truly. It's not that…" Her smile was still shaky. "I know I'm being silly but—"

"You are never silly, Maureen. Tell me, what is it I can do to ease your mind?"

"Just to be on the safe side, just so I'll feel better, could you just check my account? I know you've been having some problems with your computers, so if you could just check—"

"But of course." Standing up, Ali glanced at Faith. "Is there a way you can get me into my computer so I can check a balance?"

Faith was so stunned by the affection between Ali

and this woman, it took a moment for her to realize he was speaking to her.

"Faith?"

"I'm sorry." She jumped to her feet. "Of course." She crossed the room to his desk and booted up his computer. "Ali, can you put your password in?"

He came around the desk, stopping so close to her their bodies were touching. His masculine scent, his warmth seemed to radiate from him to her. Her pulse sped up and she felt a quick flash of heat, fire.

Her throat went dry while her palms grew damp. Absently, she wiped them down her jeans and shifted her weight away from him, so that they were no longer touching. She couldn't seem to think when he was touching her.

Quickly, with great concentration, Ali tapped in a few letters, then glanced at her, his eyes dark, intent, as if he too had felt the flash of heat between them.

With nervous fingers, Faith plugged in the code that opened the correct accounting program, quickly bringing up the accounts. "I'm sorry, your last name is Jourdan?" She glanced at Maureen.

"Yes."

Faith spelled it out to be certain she typed it in accurately. A screen popped up with Maureen and Alfred Jourdan's names at the top. Faith didn't want to look, or pry, but she would have had to have been blind not to see the amount of money in the account.

She glanced up at Ali. His face was cool, calm, serene. She glanced back at the screen. Something didn't add up. Perhaps there was another account. She punched in another set of numbers, but no other files were found.

Concerned because she'd been privy to their conversation, Faith looked curiously at Ali once again. He met her gaze levelly, as if willing her not to speak. It was not her place, or her business, so she said nothing, stepping back so he could view the computer screen.

Ali retrieved a pair of reading glasses from his pocket and leaned down to examine the screen for a moment.

"There now, see?" With a delighted smile, he straightened, then hit the button that would close it before anyone else could view the figures. "There is more than enough money to cover whatever expenses you and Alfred have. I'm sorry you haven't gotten a statement yet this month."

"Posh, Ali, you know I can never read or understand those blasted things. That's why I tell you to keep them and do it for me."

"Yes, I know, dear." He replaced his reading glasses in his pocket. "So now will you please stop worrying?" He chuckled. "Pretty soon you may have more money than me."

The woman laughed in relief, putting a hand to her heart. "Thank you, Ali." She expelled a deep breath. "I knew I'd feel better if I stopped to see you." She smiled. "You do always calm me down."

He went to her, helped her to her feet, then handed her her cane. "Now, if I promise to come to dinner next week, do you promise to stop worrying?"

She paused at the double door. "I promise." She leaned up and kissed his cheek again. "Thank you, Ali. I don't know what I would do without you."

"Probably find another man to charm." He lifted

her hand for a kiss. "And you are most welcome."
He opened the double doors to walk her out. "Now,
give my love to Alfred, tell him I'll stop by on Friday
for another game, but this time I intend to win."

"Don't count on it, Ali," she said with a laugh.
"In some things he hasn't lost his touch." There was
a sad wistfulness in her voice.

Faith stood behind Ali's desk, confused, concerned,
waiting for him to return.

"You lied to her," she accused the moment he
closed the doors behind him.

If he was surprised by her accusation, he didn't
show it. "Yes, Faith, I did." His voice was so calm,
so complacent.

"But you said she was a dear friend."

"*That* was not a lie, Faith." He went to the windows to draw the drapes against the heat of the late
afternoon sun. "She is a very dear friend." He turned
to her. "And a client."

Faith cocked her head, anger simmering just below
the surface. "Do you always lie to your clients?" The
mere thought appalled her.

His eyes darkened dangerously as he turned to her.
"No," he said slowly, carefully. "Of course I do
not."

"Could have fooled me." Fists clenched at her
side, Faith shook her head, trying to comprehend his
actions. It seemed to confirm her worst suspicions of
him, and for some reason left her surprisingly disap-
pointed. "You told her she had more than enough
money when she barely has ten thousand dollars in
her account."

"No Faith, that is not what I said to her. You were
not listening carefully."

"I was right here, I heard what you told her." Her voice edged upward in anger. "You said—"

"I *said* that there was more than enough money to take care of any needs she or Alfred might have." His voice was deathly quiet, his eyes oddly intent on her, making her shiver.

Fury nearly had her shaking. "But you know darn well that was a lie. She hardly has enough money to get through a few months." Faith couldn't prevent the outrage in her voice. She couldn't believe he could be so casually careless about something so important to someone he cared about.

It wasn't just callous, it was cruel. And it infuriated her.

Her fists clenched at her side as she took another step closer. "Obviously Maureen Jourdan is someone you care a great deal about, and she obviously cares for you. Why and how could you lie to her?" Her simmering temper erupted into a full boil. "What kind of a man are you?"

Dark emotion swept over his face and he, too, stepped closer until they were nearly standing toe to toe.

Inches taller, he seemed to be looming over her with his powerful, dark presence.

Faith refused to back down, refused to take a step back, refused to allow him to get away with something so perfectly cruel, so inhumane, it brought tears to her eyes.

Perhaps because it hit too close to home and to her ever-fragile heart.

She knew from experience what it was like to have someone you loved, depended on, lie to you, tell you they would take care of you, tell you there was more than enough money for whatever your needs, and then find out that it was lies. All lies.

Devastation was a word that could barely cover the desperation such lies created.

Like her father, apparently Ali didn't consider the consequences of his behavior, or his lies on others.

"Be careful, Faith," Ali warned in a voice that made her shiver. Instinctively, Faith ran her hands up and down her chilled arms.

Tilting her chin to meet his gaze, her eyes blazed at him. "Why, because you don't like to hear the truth? Because someone knows exactly what you are?" It wasn't hard to recognize him; it was like looking at her father all over again.

"Be careful, Faith," he warned again in a slow, low voice that almost made her take a protective step back. But Faith refused to back down, refused to cower. She'd been forced to do it once in her life; she'd not ever allow another man's lies to reduce her to that again.

Ali took several slow, deep breaths in order to control the feelings swirling inside, ready to erupt. No one had ever *dared* speak to him in such a manner. Not ever. Nor had anyone ever accused him of such unspeakable behavior before, and he found that it caused a near volcanic eruption inside of him.

His father, in his ultimate wisdom, had taught him at an early age to control his temper, which could be a vicious thing if unleashed.

And right now the leash was straining.

"Son, a man who cannot control his temper can never be in control of himself, can never truly be a man."

He heard his father's words, but at the moment,

they rang hollow and empty through his mind, his memory.

Looking at Faith, he realized what she thought of him, what she'd accused him of, and it angered him as nothing had in a long while.

He was a man who prided himself on his integrity and character. He had been taught that integrity, character and a man's name were the three most important assets a man could possess. Something no amount of money could buy, something to protect, treasure and value. He had worked hard his entire adult life to build and maintain all three.

He could not remember the last time someone had questioned his integrity. Especially a woman. No one would *dare*. No one but Faith.

It angered him, and yes, hurt just a bit because it mattered what she thought of him and he had no idea why.

"What kind of man do you think I am?" He parroted her question back to her, his voice filled with the emotion he was struggling to contain.

Faith merely blinked at him, trying not to respond to his closeness, his temper, his presence. In spite of her anger at him, he was a powerful man, and that blatant power radiated from him like sun off a sidewalk.

If she was a woman who could be intimidated, she'd be quaking in her shoes right now. A host of conflicting feelings battered her, but anger and disappointment ruled.

Ali nodded. "I see." He held up his hand as she opened her mouth to speak. "I believe your eyes tell me all I need to know." He hesitated, letting his gaze travel over her face, seeing the sadness, the tears in her eyes.

Though her words had been sharp, her face was pained. Something inside of him reacted instinctively.

She was angry, but she was also hurt. At the moment, she did not look strong and capable, but fragile and more than a little vulnerable. It tugged at something deep inside, making him want to comfort her, to ease whatever ache had put that pain in her eyes.

What had caused such despair in her, he wondered idly.

"I am sorry, Faith, that your opinion of me is so low." His words softened and his gaze stayed on hers. "It is most regrettable." He took a slow, deep breath. "But since you obviously have such a low opinion of me, perhaps you would prefer that I hire someone else to complete this job?"

Panic clutched her heart, sweeping away other emotions. She was counting on the funds this job would bring in, and cursed her tongue.

Mentally, she gave herself a shake. What Ali did and said to his friends and clients was none of her concern. If he wanted to lie until his nose grew so big he had to back into a room, that was his business. Not hers.

She was supposed to remain detached from him, and her own emotions.

But from the moment she'd laid eyes on him she knew he'd had an uncommon effect on her both physically and emotionally.

Who he was, what he represented to her had caused her to react emotionally in a way that was so unlike her.

The impact he had on her, the reaction he caused,

the feelings and emotions he aroused on a totally different plane—on a man-to-woman level—terrified her in a way nothing had in a long, long time.

Perhaps that was why she had such a difficult time remaining detached.

She knew these things, and had hoped that she could simply ignore them and go about her business without letting them interfere.

She'd been wrong.

She'd promised herself she'd stay uninvolved and unemotional. She'd just broken her own rules, and now it might cost her this job.

"Are you firing me?" she asked carefully, cursing the small catch in her voice.

Consciously, she forced herself to take a deep breath and to relax, uncurling her fists. She was suddenly so tense, the muscles in her neck were cramped.

"I am not." His gaze never left hers. She could not read the emotion that darkened his eyes. "I am merely asking if perhaps you would prefer not to work for me because I am obviously so…repugnant to you."

Guilt washed over her like a steady rain, and Faith immediately felt contrite. "I'm sorry." With a weary sigh, she pushed a few strands of hair off her cheek, struggling for control. "I don't find you repugnant, Ali." Her voice was soft and she realized she spoke the truth. "And I apologize if I gave you that impression. It's really none of my concern how you run your business."

"True."

"It's just…" She paused, at a loss to explain her feelings.

"Sometimes, Faith," he said softly, unable to resist

stroking a finger down her cheek, brushing aside a wayward strand of hair, "a lie is not necessarily a bad thing."

The impact of his words, words she'd heard so many times as a child had her insides trembling.

So he admitted he didn't think lying to someone he cared about was a bad thing. His words merely confirmed her worst fears about him.

Raw disappointment etched a place in her heart, right alongside the one her father had carved so many years ago.

It was none of her business, she reminded herself firmly. It was no concern of hers what he did or who he hurt or who he lied to. She needed this job, and she had no desire to anger him further.

"Well, if there's nothing else, I'd better get back to work." She wanted to get away from him, to forget the scene she just witnessed. To put him and his damning words and deeds out of her mind.

Realizing that he could say nothing further on the subject, Ali nodded in agreement. "Thank you for bringing me up to date. I will have Kadid make certain you have everything you need in order to get started first thing in the morning."

"Fine." She stepped around him, went to the table and gathered her notes, then walked toward the doors. She didn't look back at him, she couldn't. She didn't want him to see the tears she couldn't hold back any longer.

Three

"**M**s. Faith, I apologize for disturbing you." Kadid stood in the doorway of the sprawling room that held the entire systems operations for El-Etra Investments.

The walls and floors were a rather utilitarian gray, computer towers, monitors and printers in various states of disarray dotted every square foot of desk space. The hum of machines filtered through the air.

"May I come in, please?" he asked politely.

Turning from the computer she was working on, Faith managed a smile at the tray he carried. There was a glass full of ice, several cans of cola and a sandwich. "Of course."

"I took the liberty of having the chef prepare a little something for you." He set the tray down on the desk next to her, nudging aside a keyboard she'd disconnected.

"Bless you." She eyed the tray greedily.

"If it is not to your liking, I will be happy to have him prepare something else."

"You have a chef here?" she asked, picking up one half of the delectable-looking sandwich and taking a bite. She nearly swooned. It was the first bit of food she'd had all day and it was way past the dinner hour.

"But of course," he said with a smile. "May I?" At her nod, he lifted the can of cola and began to pour it over the glass of ice for her. "Sheik El-Etra brought him with him when he came to America. He has been with the family for almost two generations." Kadid set the empty can down on the tray. "Sheik El-Etra is a very loyal man."

The respectful tone of his voice and his careful words gave her the impression he was trying to tell her something.

"Loyal, huh?" She chewed thoughtfully. That wasn't quite the word she'd have chosen for Ali after the scene they'd had yesterday afternoon. She leaned back against her chair, deciding to take a break. "Kadid, who is Mrs. Jourdan?"

He handed her the icy glass of cola, then clasped his hands together in front of him. "She is a very old and very dear friend of the sheik's. He is not only greatly fond of her, but enormously grateful to her."

Faith frowned. "Grateful?" This didn't make sense. "Why is Ali grateful to her?"

Kadid was thoughtful. "When the sheik first came to America, he was only sixteen years old. There was political unrest in our country, and as an only son and heir and a descendant of the royal family, there was of course enormous concern for his safety, so his father sent him to America."

"To live with the Coltons."

"Yes," Kadid said with a slow nod. "Although English is a required language for all school children, Ali's English was not…shall we say, perfect." His wrinkled face creased into a smile. "As you know, children, particularly children of that age, can be cruel to anyone who is not the same as they are." He shrugged his shoulders. "The sheik was a foreigner, of royal blood, and not used to the language, customs or ways of your beautiful country."

Intrigued, Faith reached for the other half of her sandwich. "Go on."

"It was a…difficult time. He was at a very vulnerable age, an age when a boy is struggling to become a man, to show his strength, to develop his pride, and it was most difficult to be the object of cruelty."

"People were cruel to Ali?"

Having been the butt of cruelty herself as a child, Faith had grown to abhor any hint of cruelty toward anyone.

Kadid nodded sadly. "Yes, I'm afraid so. The sheik has always kept his own counsel. As a member of the royal family, it is of course expected, accepted—"

"But you knew?"

His wrinkled face once again creased into a smile. "Yes. I have been with the sheik since his birth and perhaps know him as well as his father. It is the honor of my life."

"So where does Mrs. Jourdan come in?"

"Mr. Colton was aware of the difficulties the sheik

was having. Mrs. Jourdan was a teacher at the private school where the sheik had been enrolled. Mr. Colton had heard that Mrs. Jourdan did private tutoring. She was a much-beloved, much-respected member of the community, as well as an excellent teacher, kind, loving, nurturing. With Ali's father's permission, Mr. Colton made arrangements to hire Mrs. Jourdan to help the sheik with the language, as well as with the difficult cultural adjustment he was having.''

"Maureen Jourdan was his teacher?" Faith asked in some surprise.

"Ahhh, but not just his teacher. She was that, yes," he said with a slow nod and a sly smile, "but over the years, she became so much more to the young sheik. She became his mentor, his friend, and in his mother's absence, a substitute mother. She taught him not just the language, but how do you say..." He seemed to search for the right word. "The lingo of your country and the ways of your culture." He smiled again, revealing very white teeth. "The Big Apple." He covered his mouth to hide a chuckle. "We had heard this expression, of course, but we thought this was merely a large piece of fruit." He shook his head at his own foolishness and Faith thought about her trying to explain her *Wizard of Oz* reference to Ali yesterday. Now it made sense.

She never thought about how difficult American pop culture or slang language could be for someone who had not been born in America.

"Mrs. Jourdan became the sheik's biggest supporter and of course a surrogate mother to the young, and at times, very frightened young man. She encouraged him, taught him, believed in him, and yes, loved him. As he in turn grew to love her.''

Intrigued, Faith listened, chewing thoughtfully.

''It was Mrs. Jourdan who instilled in Sheik Ali the confidence to know that one day he could return to your country, and start his business. She believed in him so much, in fact, that when he did return to America nearly ten years later, to open this business, she was his first investor.''

Finished with her sandwich, Faith was thoughtful as she reached for her cola, offering the unopened one to Kadid. Something didn't add up.

''So why would Ali lie to her if he cares so much for her?''

Kadid's dusky skin all but paled and his slender body stiffened as if she'd offended him. ''You must be mistaken, Ms. Faith.'' His white head shook slowly. ''Sheik El-Etra would never lie to anyone, let alone to Mrs. Jourdan.''

''Kadid,'' she said carefully. ''I was there. I heard him lie to her face. He told her that she would never have to worry about Alfred's— By the way, who is Alfred?'' she asked with a frown, taking a greedy sip of her icy soda.

''Mrs. Jourdan's beloved husband.'' Kadid sighed sadly. ''Mr. Jourdan is suffering from an incurable illness, one that requires constant care and round-the-clock hospitalization. It is such a pity, and pains the sheik deeply.''

''Kadid, I heard Ali tell Mrs. Jourdan that she would never have to worry about her or Alfred's expenses, when in fact the woman has barely ten thousand dollars. He lied to her.'' Her voice held the venomous emotions she'd been trying to bury since yesterday afternoon.

He looked totally perplexed. "But that is not a lie, Ms. Faith. It is the truth." Relieved, his shoulders seemed to relax. "Mrs. Jourdan will never have to worry about any expenses, medical or otherwise."

"On ten thousand dollars?" One brow rose. "Come on, Kadid, this is America. Do you have any idea what round-the-clock medical care in a first-class facility costs?" Because of the cost, her mother had to go to a state-run hospital.

Kadid looked perplexed. "But it does not matter Ms. Faith. The sheik personally takes care of all of their expenses and always will."

"Wait." Shaking her head, she held up her hand. Her headache had suddenly returned. "Are you telling me the sheik uses his own money to pay for Alfred's care and Mrs. Jourdan's living expenses?"

"But of course. The sheik is a loyal, honorable man. His deep affection and gratitude toward Mrs. Jourdan cannot be measured in dollars. She gave him so much, he feels it is his privilege to be able to give something—even something as insignificant as money—in return. He feels it is an honor for him to do so."

Speechless, and feeling slightly sick to her stomach, Faith recalled her conversation with Ali yesterday, recalled her accusations, her condemnation.

He'd never defended himself, never said a word. He'd simply let her go on thinking... She glanced at Kadid and was heartily afraid she was going to lose her lunch.

"Oh, Kadid," she moaned.

"Are you ill?" Alarmed, he placed a gentle hand on her shoulder. "Shall I phone the sheik's physician?" He patted her back nervously. "He can be here momentarily."

"No," she said weakly, mortified, humiliated, and more embarrassed than she'd ever been in her life. "I'm not ill, just an idiot."

"No, Ms. Faith." He patted her back. "Most certainly you are not an idiot."

"Yes, I am." She glanced up at him. "Kadid, I accused Ali of all kinds of things. Basically called him a liar and—"

"You called Sheik Ali a liar?" Kadid's eyes had bulged. "Oh dear." He clasped his hands together. "Oh." He sighed. Loudly. "Dear."

"Exactly." Miserable, Faith shut down the computer she'd been working on, knowing she'd never be able to concentrate now. It was late in the day, and she was totally drained, partially because she'd been in an outrageous emotional uproar ever since her confrontation with Ali yesterday.

Miserable, she pushed the keyboard across the table so she could rest her head on her hands for a moment.

"Kadid." She lifted her head. "Why on earth— Never mind. I think I understand." She wasn't exactly sure she did understand anything about this, except that she'd made a complete and total fool out of herself. "So Mrs. Jourdan was a mentor and surrogate mother to Ali, so that's why he's grateful, and why he's doing what he's doing."

"Yes. Mrs. Jourdan is more than just a mentor, or a surrogate mother. Ten years ago, when the sheik returned to America, it was she who helped him get over the heartbreak of Jalila's death—''

Faith's head came up. "Wait a minute. Who's Jalila?''

Kadid hesitated. "Forgive me, Ms. Faith. I spoke out of turn. I should not have—''

"No, please.'' She touched his arm. "Kadid, it's important to me. Who is Jalila?''

He sighed, looking torn. Finally he sighed again. "She was the sheik's intended.''

"Intended what?'' Faith asked with a frown.

Kadid struggled to find the right words to explain. "They were betrothed.'' He searched for another word. "They were to be married.''

"Ali was going to be married?'' She had a hard time envisioning the playboy whose picture she saw in the paper almost every morning, sporting a new woman like a shiny, new toy, with a man who would settle down with just *one* woman. "What happened?'' she asked softly.

Kadid stared straight ahead for a long moment before finally speaking. "After his schooling, the sheik returned home to prepare for his wedding. It was to be a joyous, gala celebration for the family, and the country.'' His voice was soft, echoing with sadness. "Three weeks before the wedding, Jalila was killed when a buried landmine exploded under her vehicle. She was killed instantly.'' He took a deep breath, then let it out slowly. "That was ten years ago.''

"Is that why Ali came to America?''

He nodded. "Yes. That is when he decided to start his business.''

She nodded, realizing the puzzle pieces were starting to fit. "And when Mrs. Jourdan became his customer and why he's so grateful to her." No wonder there was so much love and affection between them.

Kadid smiled, pleased that she seemed to understand. "Yes, that is correct."

"Kadid?" Frowning, Faith tried to digest all this information. It threw a serious crimp in the image and the opinion she'd had of Ali. "Are there many others that the sheik is grateful to?"

Kadid's chin lifted and he stared straight ahead. "The sheik is a kind and generous man who has many, many friends."

Lord, it was getting worse by the minute, Faith thought with a soft groan.

"The sheik is a man who believes strongly in loyalty to those who have honored him with their friendship and their trust."

Faith closed her eyes again, the entire scene with Maureen Jourdan replaying over and over in her mind. Something Mrs. Jourdan said was confusing and she'd forgotten to ask Ali about it. Now, after what Kadid had told her, her curiosity was even more aroused. "Kadid?"

"Yes, Ms. Faith?"

"When Ali introduced me to Mrs. Jourdan, she said something about his parents' taste in women improving. What was she talking about?"

Kadid seemed to hesitate. "Sheik Ali is an only son. It is his duty and obligation to marry and produce an heir."

"Okay, fine. So he's got to marry and produce a son. What does that have to do with me or his parents?"

"With you, I'm afraid I am not certain," he admitted with a bit of a frown. "Sheik Ali's parents have been concerned over his apparent lack of success in finding a suitable bride. Since Jalila's death he has not had a serious relationship and it greatly concerns his parents."

"I can imagine." Faith smiled. "The man does go through women like a revolving door."

"For the past several years, the sheik's parents have been pressuring him to find a proper wife, and when he did not, they took it upon themselves to start…arranging dates for him with appropriately suitable women."

Faith's eyes narrowed and she held up her hand. "Wait a minute. Are you telling me this bevy of beauties he's with every night are women his parents have fixed him up with because they want him to settle down and get married?"

Kadid nodded. "Yes."

"Why the heck doesn't he just tell them no?"

Kadid smiled. "Ms. Faith, the sheik is extremely close to his parents. His love for them knows no bounds. Family is very important to Sheik Ali. And his parents' intentions are honorable and meant to be helpful. To tell his parents that he does not wish for them to help him find or choose a mate would be disrespectful and perhaps hurtful, something the sheik would never do."

"I see," Faith said dully, realizing that apparently there was a whole lot she really didn't see.

At least not about Sheik Ali El-Etra. She was going to have to rethink her entire opinion of him.

"Are you finished with your meal, Ms. Faith?" Kadid was reaching for the now empty tray.

Thoughts churning, Faith merely nodded. "Yes, Kadid." She had to swallow, but her throat felt like a boulder was stuck in it. "Thank you very much for being so thoughtful. I was starving."

He smiled. "I cannot take credit for your meal, Ms. Faith. Sheik Ali asked me to please see to it that the chef prepared something for you since he was pretty certain you had not taken the time to eat today." He lifted the tray, sliding her empty soft drink cans onto it. "Can I get you anything else?" He reached for her empty plate, placed it on the tray. "Some dessert perhaps?"

Faith shook her head. "Not unless that chef of yours has some crow cookies."

The music was soft and slow, the lights subdued, the champagne imported and very, very cold.

Bored, Ali stood in the back of the glittering ballroom, letting his eyes wander across the crowded floor, praying his date for the evening—Candy or Cookie or whatever her name was—would keep herself busy for a few minutes to give him some blissful peace from her endless chattering.

With a deep sigh, Ali realized in spite of his annoyance at his date, he could not gather any anger for his parents, and their infernal, eternal matchmaking.

Tonight had turned out to be another disaster. But his parents meant well, and their actions were done out of a sense of deep love for him, a love that he returned tenfold.

Usually he found their mismatching endearing and slightly amusing.

But not tonight.

Tonight, he was too disturbed to be amused by the company of a beautiful, but vacuous woman whose only interest in life was the increasing size of her breasts and decreasing the size of his bank account.

He couldn't help but compare her to Faith. He had not stopped thinking about her, or the rather rancid encounter they'd had yesterday afternoon.

In spite of his annoyance, he caught himself smiling. Faith, who showed such passion for all that she did, for everything in her life. She was a woman who had and displayed genuine feelings. Anger. Impatience. Annoyance. And even disappointment.

With a frown, he thought of their conversation again, thought of it, and regretted it. He couldn't help but wonder what he had done to give her such a terrible opinion of him.

Perhaps, he mused, as he sipped his mineral water and breathed a grateful sigh as his date was snagged by Ronald Preston for a walk on the terrace, Faith merely disliked men.

No, he couldn't believe that. She was far too passionate about everything to turn her back on a relationship. No, he had a feeling it was him in particular she didn't care for, and he couldn't help but wonder why.

He was certain most women found him rather pleasant to be around, fawning and falling all over him. Faith, on the other hand, treated him with a suspicious air, as if he was about to snatch her purse and make off with its contents. The contrast was so drastic, so distinct, he could not help but find it both annoying and amusing.

Faith was quite simply an enigma, unlike any woman he had ever known.

She was a self-sufficient, independent woman who obviously did not care one whit about fashion or his bank account. In fact, she actually seemed offended by his wealth.

Nothing like the women his parents were constantly trying to fix him up with.

He had known since birth that he had a responsibility and obligation to marry and produce an heir.

But he would do so, not out of obligation or responsibility, but out of loyalty and respect for his parents. It was expected, required, yes, but family meant far too much to him to do anything merely to uphold a tradition.

Although he'd been Kuwati born, and of royal blood, he had spent so much of his formative youth in America, that he'd distanced himself from the more traditional beliefs of his countrymen.

While it was traditional in his homeland and, at times, still expected to have one's marriage arranged—particularly for those who had social, political and economic responsibilities—he was not a man who could accept or abide by an empty marriage no matter what his responsibilities.

But he had had the love of his life once, and knew that he would not risk his heart to another again. He could not, for he could never allow his heart to be at risk again.

It had almost killed him when Jalila had been killed. He had loved her totally, completely, with his

heart and soul, and knew that they would have a wonderful future, a wonderful life, and marriage.

He had no desire to ever love that deeply, that desperately again.

But he had an old-fashioned belief that a man was
meant to have an equal partner, a mate to share all of
life's joys and sorrows.

But he did not want just a paper marriage, with a
beautiful vacuous woman, a marriage that was merely
an obligation, legally binding, but morally, physically
and emotionally bankrupt. Such a thing would be not
only dishonest, but an affront to his own personal
integrity.

No, he wanted a partner, an equal, a woman he
could respect, care for, but one he would never love.

Because of his position, he needed a bright, intelligent woman who was her own person, with her own
thoughts, goals and ideals. Qualities that complemented and enhanced her femininity.

A woman who was not impressed by what he had,
but by who he was. A woman who could see past all
of the material objects in his life that were necessary
and expected because of his title, to the flesh and
blood man beneath it all.

A woman who would settle for a marriage without
the deepest commitment of love. She could have all
that he had; she just could never have his heart.

Not such an unpleasant situation, really. They
would have a stable, secure marriage, steeped in respect, mutual interests, passion and intelligence without all the bothersome emotional details that could
entangle a relationship and strangle it.

Although his parents' marriage had been arranged,

they had become true life partners, partners who respected each other and had made a wonderful life together. Love had never entered the picture; perhaps that was why his parents' marriage had succeeded so well.

Ali sighed, sipping his drink. Unfortunately, until he found a suitable bride, his parents would continue to fix him up with the daughters and cousins and nieces of friends, hoping against hope that one would be the right fit.

And he realized that out of his deep sense of loyalty and love for his parents, he would simply have to accept it.

But that didn't mean he had to like it.

With a sigh, Ali let his gaze wander across the dance floor. He lifted his glass to take a sip, and his arm froze halfway as he spotted a familiar redhead on the dance floor.

Faith.

Ali turned, setting his glass down on the bar, so he could move closer, narrowing his gaze on her partner.

Aaron Josslyn. Ali's brows drew together in a concerned frown. The man drank far too much, and had a reputation for treating women roughly, but because of his parents' wealth, Aaron's behavior was commonly overlooked.

Ali skirted the dance floor so he could watch them.

His mouth went dry as the desert of his homeland as his gaze took Faith in.

While other women wore glittering jewels, her body was completely unadorned. Most of the gowns this evening were bright, vivid, low-cut or skintight, revealing much more than they attempted to conceal.

Among them, Faith stood out like a proud, elegant eagle among a yard of preening peacocks. Her gown was black, simple, sleeveless and high-necked. It drifted in layers to the floor, floating over that heavenly, lush, body in a way that would make a healthy man's loin's ache.

Her hair was down tonight, falling free and wild in a riot of fiery curls that caressed the beautiful, feminine curve of her shoulders, framing her face like a rich, amber halo.

He couldn't take his eyes off her. And neither, apparently, could Aaron.

Or his hands.

As they turned, Ali caught a glimpse of Faith's face as Aaron began to paw her on the dance floor. She was white, with twin spots of color on her cheeks, and her eyes were wide.

Ali's vision hazed as he felt a hand of anger clutch his gut. He'd never considered himself a jealous man; he'd never had the opportunity to experience the emotion. But now it seized him by the throat, nearly knocking the wind out of him.

He had learned from his father how to control his emotions, to behave in the respectable, gentlemanly fashion befitting his position.

The emotions tearing through him right now were neither respectable nor gentlemanly.

Without taking his eyes off them, Ali crossed the dance floor toward them.

"May I cut in?" Although his voice was low and polite, it vibrated with anger as he clamped a hand down hard on Aaron's shoulder.

"Go away." Aaron didn't even bother to glance at

him, but kept his attention on Faith, who was now openly struggling to free herself from Aaron.

Still smiling, Ali tightened his fingers on the man's shoulder until he winced.

"Hey, this is my dance and I'm not done." Aaron's words were slightly slurred as he tightened his arms around Faith, dragging her closer. "Get lost!"

"Aaron!" Pressing her hands to his chest, Faith tried to arch away.

Ali didn't wait. With one quick movement of his hand, he knocked Aaron's arms away from Faith, then moved between them, sweeping her into the protective embrace of his arms, putting his body between her and Aaron.

"Hey, what the hell do you think you're doing?" Aaron's voice rose in the crowded room; thankfully it was drowned out by the strains of the song. He reached for Ali, who whirled on him.

His face was a fiery mask of venomous rage. "You're drunk, Aaron. Go home while you can still walk of your own accord." Ali grabbed the lapels of the man's tux and dragged him closer, nearly lifting him off the floor.

Aaron's eyes bulged in their sockets, and his Adam's apple danced up and down.

"One more word out of you and I regret to say you will need an ambulance to take you home." Ali's voice was low and controlled so as not to alarm the other guests. A scene would only further embarrass Faith. "Now get out of here."

Ali released the man so abruptly, he stumbled. Then Aaron scrambled off the dance floor, pushing his way through other couples.

"Are you all right?" Ali asked, gently taking Faith in his arms again and smoothly leading her around the dance floor as if there had been no incident.

"Ali." Her voice held a bit of relief as her arms instinctively went around him. She nearly sagged against him. "Thank you. I'm fine, really."

He drew back to look at her, his face concerned. "You're trembling." He could easily thrash Aaron Josslyn without a second thought. The man was a barbarian.

"I—I know." She glanced at up him, surprised by how relieved she was to see him. "I'm all right, really. I was more angry than frightened. He's an idiot, but I didn't want to create a scene." Discreetly she glanced around, relieved to see no one seemed to be paying the least bit of attention to her.

Ali smiled. "Yes, I understand." He held her lightly, gently, but beneath his hands he could feel the warmth of her skin beneath her gown, feel the press of her curves against his chest.

His blood stirred, heated at her closeness, at the knowledge of her body pressed so closely, so intimately against his.

She was close enough now that he finally caught a brief hint of her scent. It was something incredibly feminine and subtle, something familiar, yet he could not put a name on it.

It was not an expensive French perfume, for he recognized almost every one of the overpowering scents of the imported fragrances.

No, this was something far too delicate, like a whispered memory one couldn't quite recall, the kind that stayed with you for a while, yet had enough of a kick to heat a man's blood and his imagination, making him wonder if her body carried that scent all over.

He had a feeling it would be a pleasure to find out. "Are you sure you're all right?" He tilted her chin up, saw the shadows in her eyes.

His breath tickled the small tendrils of hair framing her cheeks, causing goose bumps to rise and her heart to scamper like a terrified rabbit.

She had to swallow hard before she spoke because her mouth had gone dry at his touch, at the tender look in his eyes.

"Y-Yes, really, Ali, thank you." She glanced away. He was too close, and the intensity of his closeness was too much. "I appreciate what you did."

She didn't want to admit she wasn't trembling as much from Aaron's ridiculous groping as she was from the fact that Ali was holding her intimately.

Ali glanced behind him to be certain Aaron was gone. "The man is a rude, arrogant fool who should not be allowed out in public."

"And those are probably his good points," she teased, glancing up at him, trying to break the sudden tension quivering between them.

She couldn't believe how the man looked in a tuxedo. It was probably illegal to look that good, she decided, realizing that in spite of her own reservations and cautions, she wasn't immune to Ali's incredible good looks or unbelievable charm.

Faith sighed. So, she was human, at least she could admit her appreciation for the male species, this male in particular, without losing her head. Maybe that was a healthy thing.

Swaying with him to the soft strains of the music,

Faith glanced up at him. "What are you doing here, Ali?"

He shrugged. "The host is one of my clients." Smiling, Ali nodded in greeting to another couple who danced by. "I try to attend as many of my clients' functions as I can. It is good for business."

She laughed. "Some business. The tickets to this gig were five thousand dollars apiece."

He shrugged. "It is for a worthwhile charity, Faith, and I believe good causes deserve our support." Amused, and delighted to have her in his arms, he studied her face, noted in spite of her formal attire she did not have on a bit of makeup. She'd never looked lovelier. "And you, Faith? What are you doing here?"

"Besides arm-wrestling with an ape?" She laughed. "Mr. Josslyn invited me. The Senior Mr. Josslyn," she clarified. "I've been trying to land his account for several months." She frowned, trying to concentrate on the dance steps. Ali's closeness, the scent she now recognized as only his, and the intensity of his gaze were making her nervous, causing her to lose her concentration. "He asked me to come this evening. It's the only night he's in town and he said we'd have a few minutes to meet."

"And have you met with him?" His glanced at her unpainted mouth. It looked unbearably inviting, and he thought of his first impression of her the first day they'd met—she had a mouth made for kissing and kissing well. A well of warmth unfurled low in his gut, causing him to tighten his hand on hers, wanting to hold her closer.

"Unfortunately, no. Something came up at the last

minute and he couldn't make it." His hand was very soft, very gentle, yet strong, masculine. The kind of hand that could soothe or arouse.

For an instant Faith wondered what it would feel like to have that hand warm her in other places. Female places. The thought made her blood seem to heat and pump faster through her veins.

"Do not concern yourself about it." Ali flashed her a glorious smile that nearly made her stumble. She forced herself to concentrate on her feet and the dance steps as he led her around the crowded dance floor.

"I have known Abner Josslyn for a long, long time. We have been partners in several ventures over the years. Once I tell him what a marvelous job you have done for El-Etra Investments, I'm sure there will be no problem arranging a proper meeting."

Touched, she tried to hide the joy that stole through her at his words. A sterling recommendation from Ali would go a long way toward cementing her firm's growing reputation.

"That's very generous of you," she said softly. "And kind. I appreciate it very much considering the things I said to you yesterday afternoon."

"The truth is not much to appreciate," he said with a laugh.

Tilting her head, she met his dark gaze head-on. He was making her feel things, things she could no longer ignore. "Ali, why didn't you tell me about Maureen Jourdan yesterday?" Curious, she watched several emotions play across his chiseled features as he seemed to ponder her question.

Finally, he spoke. "Faith, in the first place, it would be unethical for me to discuss a client's financial situation with you or anyone else. I am in a fiduciary capacity. As such, my clients trust me to preserve and maintain their privacy, as I'm sure you understand.''

"Of course, but—''

He pressed a finger to her lips to silence her, letting it linger there for a long moment as his gaze caressed her face. A shiver stole over her.

''I would never betray a confidence, Faith, not of a client, not of a friend, not of anyone. Such a thing is totally foreign to me.'' He saw the suspicion cloud her eyes again but this time only for a brief moment.

''In spite of what you may think of me, integrity, honor and respect are all integral parts of my life.'' He smiled a slow, seductive smile that made her blood race. ''Blame it on my parents.'' He shrugged. ''It is how they raised me.''

Confused, she shook her head. ''But you stood there and let me accuse you of lying to her, to me. You allowed me to...'' Faith's voice trailed off and she realized how ludicrous she sounded.

Her eyes slid closed. Good Lord. He hadn't *let her* do anything. She'd done it all on her own.

''I owe you an apology,'' she said softly, unaware that she was arching against him, pressing closer to him to feel the warmth radiating from him. ''The things I said...'' Ashamed, her voice trailed off. ''They were unconscionable. I jumped to some unfair conclusions and accused you of some terrible things. What I did was unfair and unwarranted.''

''Unfair, perhaps.'' He smiled, stroking a finger down her cheek, wanting to erase the frown of worry. ''Unwarranted, not at all, Faith, not if you believed me to be the things you accused me of. I would certainly expect you to have a low opinion of me, one that I would truly deserve.''

''But you're not any of the things I accused you of, are you?'' There was something powerfully mesmerizing about his eyes.

''No,'' he said slowly, grateful that perhaps they'd finally reached some kind of watershed. ''I am not. But that of course is for you to discover and judge for yourself.'' His gaze searched hers as he continued to hold her, moving closer to bring her closer. ''And I appreciate your apology,'' he whispered. ''Sometimes admitting we are wrong is a very difficult thing.''

Faith nodded. He was beginning to shatter the entire image she'd had of him. Now she wasn't certain what to believe. And it confused and frightened her.

Who was Sheik Ali El-Etra?

Faith wasn't certain she knew, not really. But she wasn't certain she wanted to find out, either.

It was much easier to accept what she once thought him to be, easier just so that she could deny the impact he was having on her, easier so she wouldn't even have to consider the way he made her feel, feelings she'd never really had to deal with before.

They terrified her.

She was smart enough to recognize the overwhelming power of the physical attraction she felt for Ali from the moment they'd met. To deny it would have been not only ridiculous, but immature, two things she'd tried never to be.

She was an adult, and accepted and expected sensuality to be a part of her life at some point with the right man.

But definitely not now, and definitely not with *this* man, a man who made her knees weak and her head spin just by his mere presence.

A man who seemed to have the ability to reduce her to what her mother had become.

A man she believed to be so like her father it was frightening.

A man she had absolutely no intention of getting involved with on a personal level.

But for the first time in her life she *almost* understood her mother's mistakes. Until now, she'd never experienced that heady rush of overwhelming sexual desire, like a living, breathing beast waiting to devour a woman if she was not careful.

And careful was something her mother unfortunately never learned to be.

She, however, had learned from her mother's mistakes.

Her mother had kept walking into the belly of the beast over and over again, taking her father back time and time again, no matter how many times he'd lied to her, cheated on her, until Faith had lost all respect for her mother. Then came the day her gorgeous, irresponsible father had finally left for good, taking every penny they had and her mother's spirit with him.

It had been devastating for her mother. And just as devastating for a fourteen-year-old girl who had worshipped her father, a father who left her to fend for herself, and left her with a mother who emotionally fell apart at his final betrayal and had to be hospitalized, and was never, ever the same again.

It was a lesson Faith had never forgotten. A lesson

in how a woman who was not careful could get caught in a trap of her own making.

Faith knew from an early age she would never get caught in that trap.

Never depend, need or lean on a man. Never lose yourself in the emotional or physical connection to a man so that if he left, he took your joy, your spirit, your will to live with him.

From the moment she'd met Ali, Faith had secretly feared that fate had destined her to repeat her mother's mistakes.

What was it about Ali, she wondered, glancing up at him, that caused her to react so strongly?

Their eyes caught, held, and Faith's heart began a wicked thud. It was as if the music, the other guests, everything faded into the background as she merely lost herself in the depth of Ali's beautiful dark eyes.

She was suddenly so vividly aware of him and his touch, his hand at her back, the press of his chest against her breasts causing them to feel heavy, tight. The feel of his arms around her, holding, *protecting* her.

"You look enchanting this evening." His lips brushed her temple, moved to her ear, sending a ripple of sexual shock waves down to her toes.

Instinctively, she tightened her arms around him, letting her fingers caress the silky hair at the back of his neck.

Lifting a hand, he touched the fiery ends of her hair. It was as soft and silky as he imagined.

"Your hair is beautiful." He drew back to look at her again, his gaze slowly going over her face, an intense look in his eyes as they finally settled on her mouth.

Instinctively, Faith licked her dry lips, aware that Ali's gaze followed the movement of her tongue. It sent a thrill racing through her, weakening her knees.

She glanced at his mouth, that beautifully sculptured mouth. He was so close now his lips were just a heartbeat away.

She wondered what it would feel like to have that mouth on hers, hungry, demanding, fulfilling.

The thought utterly shocked her, and her palms grew damp, her body moist, as she tried to ignore the thought and focus instead on moving her feet, following his lead, but her attention kept drifting to the feel of him, his touch and what it was doing to her.

"You should wear your hair down more often," he whispered again, still watching her with those dark eyes. "It is enchanting."

"Thank you." Pressed against him, she could feel his arousal, feel the barely leashed power of his magnificent body.

Never taking his eyes off of her, Ali stroked a finger down her cheek, across her chin, lifted it to her mouth to gently, sensuously rub it against her bottom lip.

Her breath caught. She felt her reserves slip away and let her gaze linger on his lips. Her own mouth parted slightly, tingling from his touch.

She could feel her breath wither out of her; it was an effort to breathe. She wanted to taste his lips, to feel his mouth on hers. She wanted it with a desperation that shocked her.

As if sensing her desire, his arms tightened around

her, pulling her closer until there wasn't room for a breath between them.

Her guard collapsed as she tilted her head up, knowing, *wanting* him to kiss her.

"Faith." Her name was a whispered caress as he lowered his head, and gently, lightly teased her lips with his.

Fire shot through her limbs, weakening them, and she clung to him, wanting more, knowing she was going to get burned and, for the moment, not caring.

Logic deserted her, every warning she'd ever whispered to herself like a mantra evaporated as Ali's mouth, softly, sensuously moved against her, making her ache with need, with desire.

She moaned softly, desperately dragging his head down to deepen the kiss for one riotous moment of undisciplined madness. Only one moment, she told herself. It was all she'd allow herself.

His mouth came down on hers. Not gentle, not coaxing, but possessive, demanding. Claiming all that he'd wanted, desired, needed.

"Oh God." Her words were a plea, a prayer, as she threaded her fingers through the silk of his hair.

Desire, hot and hungry, shot through her system, buckling her defenses. She clung tighter, tightening her arms around him to bring him closer, to hang on as the whirlwind caught her, flinging her into the wanton world of desperate, achy desire.

Need. Sweet Lord, he'd never felt this need, this all-encompassing power to possess a woman, to claim, to put his stamp on her. He was experienced, but had never experienced this jolt of such unbridled desire, hot, dangerous, demanding to be fueled, fed, sated.

He couldn't breathe. His lungs felt as if they were filled with cotton candy. His mind clouded, his senses blurred until all that remained were feelings, the feelings Faith had aroused in him. Wild. Desperate. Frantic.

It caught Ali, stunning him, nearly blinding him with the knowledge that he could be reduced to a mass of hard, aching flesh.

And only that.

By Faith. Plain, simple Faith.

She was not the kind of woman he'd ever imagined, but this moment, in his arms, her response was all he'd ever wanted. Unbridled passion and heat, given freely, unequivocally, with an energy and desire that matched his own.

"Ali."

She moaned his name, and he took the moan with his mouth, opening it slightly, letting his tongue tease her lips, hearing her soft moan again, as she pressed all of her feminine glory against him, standing on tiptoe to return the passion that threatened to engulf them in a blazing inferno.

His hand fisted in her hair, and he tilted her head to better devour, to taste, to savor, knowing that this would never be enough.

It was like waving a pitcher of glistening ice water in front of a man perishing from thirst and telling him he could only have a sip.

One little sip.

All this kiss had done was whet his appetite for more. More of her.

"Oh God." The words came out a husky whisper. With her senses reeling, her mind spinning, Faith struggled against the feelings that engulfed her, fighting for control, for some semblance of sense.

But desire dug in, clawed for purchase, then spread through her. Her nipples hardened against the fabric of her dress, and she rubbed against him, trying to ease the sudden ache, the throbbing that made her want to scream in utter, absolute frustration.

She had been reduced to all that she'd feared her whole life by one kiss.

"Faith." He dragged her closer, trying to absorb her touch, her taste, her scent into his senses.

This was Faith, a woman who, until now, he never realized was far more powerful with her simple clothes and her plain presentation. A woman who disdained him, his title, his bloodlines and even his bank account. A woman who had more feminine power than all of the beautiful women he'd ever encountered all rolled together.

She had the power to not only touch his body but, he realized with a fear he'd not known in years, his impenetrable heart.

His breath was gone, his legs wobbly, his mind reeling with the knowledge that Faith had the power to destroy him with just a kiss. A simple kiss.

But perhaps not so simple.

A kiss that changed the way he looked at her, saw her, thought of her.

And himself.

He felt weak, vulnerable, capable of being hurt.

It frightened him as nothing had since his youth.

No woman had ever had such power over him, not since Jalila.

"Ali." Frightened, Faith pulled away from him, trying to take a breath. Her head was spinning. "We— This—" She shook her head, trying to clear it, to step out of the fog, but she was unable to put her tumbling thoughts together coherently.

Somehow the music had stopped, started again. Couples, oblivious to them on the crowded floor, danced around them.

Resolve resurfaced, and with it, the knowledge that she had done the unthinkable. The thing she'd sworn her whole life never to do.

Let physical or emotional need render her senseless. Witless.

Like her mother.

Faith glanced around and realized they were in the middle of a dance floor at an elegant black-tie gala. And she'd been standing here kissing Ali with the abandon of a sixteen-year-old.

Embarrassed, she shook her head, trying to shake some sense back into it.

"I'm sorry, this shouldn't have happened." She had to swallow. Her throat was so dry it was difficult to speak. "We...we can't do this."

Regret, sharp and deep, streaked through her. She knew this man was a danger to her. Knew it, and had walked willingly into his arms.

Just like her mother had done so many times with her father.

The thought was like a splash of cold water and Faith tried to take a step back, to put some much-needed distance between them, hoping distance would quell the heat that was still rocking her body with aftershocks.

"Can't?" Ali looked at her, his face thunderous. Can't was not a word he was used to, people rarely denied him anything. Especially a woman. How could she stand here and deny the most elemental feelings that surged so gloriously between them?

If he wasn't so aroused, so unfulfilled, so filled with longing he would have been amused that she could think such a ludicrous thought.

"I believe it is too late for *can'ts,* Faith." He reached for her again, but she stepped back, out of his reach, holding her hands in front of her like an armor.

"Like it or not, it *has* happened." He would not let her deny something that had so profoundly affected him. Could not let her deny it, not when the evidence of their passion was so visible.

Her eyes were glazed, hazy with passion, a passion he knew had not yet fully developed, or exploded. When it did, he knew it would be a beautiful thing.

Two bright spots of color touched her cheeks, and her mouth—that beautiful, glorious, sensuous mouth—was parted and slightly swollen from their kiss. He wanted to cover her mouth with his again, to sip of her sweetness, to feel her body pressed against his, to feel her heat match his.

"I want you," he said simply, slipping an arm around her slender waist to draw her closer. He couldn't bear to have her so near and yet so far. "You want me. It is not a complicated thing. Do not be afraid of what you feel, of what is between us. It is the most natural thing in the world."

"No." She shook her head, and even though her legs were shaking, she stepped out of his embrace. She wasn't afraid of what was between them—she was terrified of it to the tips of her soul.

"I *don't* want you," she lied, raising her chin and letting her gaze defiantly meet his.

He looked at her long and hard for a moment. "Your mouth tells lies your body denies, Faith." A small, sad smile touched his lips. "Who is lying now, Faith?" he asked quietly. "Who is lying now?"

Ashamed that he'd turned the tables on her, she shook her head. Desire was still roaring restlessly through her. She wanted nothing more than to walk back into his arms, to hold him.

Which was precisely why she knew she couldn't ever go back to that place she'd just visited.

Not ever. It was far too dangerous.

"I'm not lying." She wished her voice was firmer, stronger, more believable. Even to her own ears she sounded weak. It infuriated and shamed her.

"I *don't* want you." Maybe if she kept saying it, it would be so.

"Ah, but I want you." He trailed a finger sensuously down her bare arm, making her body quake, and her blood heat, wanting to prove to her, to force her to see what was between them.

She jerked back, unwilling to admit that just his slightest touch could reduce her to mush. "You can't have me."

She couldn't succumb to passion, couldn't forget all that she'd learned growing up, all the pain and heartache a man like this could bring to a woman's life. To her life.

"Oh, but I will have you, Faith," he whispered confidently, only infuriating her.

"You arrogant..." Her voice trailed off and she caught herself before she said something she knew she'd regret. Her eyes darkened. Anger quickly smothered the passion, making her realize how foolish she'd been. She welcomed the anger; it was familiar, comfortable, something she knew she could handle. "I don't know who you think you are—"

"I thought you knew." His voice had gone soft again, laced with steely determination. "I am Sheik Ali El-Etra—"

"Auggh!" She wanted to smack him. "You're gonna start with that nonsense again? Tossing your title around like I should bow to you?"

"Nonsense?" His brows drew together slowly as he tried to comprehend what she'd just said to him. No one had ever dared refer to his title as nonsense. He stiffened, his eyes narrowing dangerously. "There are those who would bow merely because of my title, Faith."

Frustrated and fuming, she blew out a breath. The man was insufferable. Arrogant and pigheaded.

"Yeah, well, I'm not one of them. I am *not* one of your beautiful bevy of the brainless. Nor am I interested in a one-night stand, I don't care who you are." Eyes shooting sparks, Faith lifted her chin. "And I have a news flash for you, *Sheik*. You may have had everything you've ever wanted in life up until now, but there's one thing you will *never* have." She gave his chest a poke, furious at the smug arrogance shimmering in his eyes. "Me."

With that, Faith turned on her heel and marched

away, leaving Ali standing in the middle of the dance floor, alone, staring after her with a perplexed look on his face.

"Ah, dear Faith, but on this too you are wrong." Slipping his hands in his pocket, he watched her sail through the doors into the cool, dark evening with a confident smile. "I *will* have you."

Four

___

Prosperino, California

In the dark, the elegant Colton estate rose like a proud, welcoming beacon atop a high, rocky cliff overlooking the Pacific Ocean.

A cool, foggy mist swirled in the evening wind, rising through the darkness, wrapping the elegant mansion in a lazy, hazy shawl.

Moonlight silhouetted the jagged cliffs and the aprons of beach scattered along the shoreline. The scent of salt and the ocean mingled with the fragrance of tea roses, dianthus and begonias from the grounds' magnificent gardens, perfuming the night air with a sweet, subtle bouquet.

Christened *Hacienda del Alegria*—House of Joy—

the sprawling Colton house had once rung with laughter and love, children and family.

But not anymore, Emily Blair Colton thought sadly, as she crossed the circular driveway at the front of the house. Now the house held more tension and sadness than anything else.

Although it was late and dark, she dreaded going home, dreaded going into the house that had once been a home.

But not any longer.

Pausing in the darkness, silhouetted by shafts of the high moon, Emily glanced up at the house that had once meant security and stability to her, the home that had once meant everything to her.

She shivered in the darkness, pulling her sweater tighter around her. Her life had changed when she was eleven.

Rubbing a throbbing spot on her temple, Emily slowly began walking, making her way up the rest of the drive toward the front entrance.

Everything in her life was now referenced by the accident.

Before the accident.

After the accident.

Before the accident her life had been blissful, happy, secure. She and her adopted mother had been so close.

She'd been a toddler when her parents had been killed and she'd been taken in as a foster child and then adopted by Joe and Meredith Colton.

Meredith had quickly nicknamed her Sparrow because of her slight frame and slender body.

With the Coltons she'd found the security and stability that had been shattered with her parents' untimely deaths, and something far more important—love.

They'd adopted her, given her their name, made her theirs. Her relationship with her new brothers and sisters, her parents, and especially her mother couldn't have been more perfect. She was once again safe, loved, protected.

Her mother, Meredith, had become the most important person in her life. She'd admired her, loved her, wanted to be just like her.

Until the accident.

Emily sighed as she started up the steps, digging in the front pocket of her shorts for her house key.

The day her life forever changed.

The morning of the accident, she and her mother had been on their way to visit Emily's grandmother when their car had been run off the road. Although neither was seriously injured, the after-effects of the accident had been devastating.

The exact details and events of that day were still fuzzy in Emily's mind, still troublesome because she couldn't remember everything. And trying to remember always brought on such blinding, vicious headaches. Lately, too, she'd been plagued by terrible nightmares.

That day had become a blur in her mind. She could remember very little of the details before she'd been brought to the emergency room, but one important detail had never left her: When she'd regained consciousness at the site, she'd seen two of her mother.

For some reason, even now, if she closed her eyes,

she could still see the two images of her mother beside the mangled car. Two identical images.

Emily blinked, rubbing her eyes, thinking the vision would go away. It didn't. When she opened her
eyes both her mothers were still there.

And for some reason, whenever she thought of the
two mothers, she thought of one as good and one as
evil.

Although she'd not been seriously injured that day,
she *had* suffered a concussion, and that was what the
doctors had blamed for her subsequent nightmares,
headaches and her misguided memories.

She'd told the doctors about seeing two of her
mother, but they brushed aside her story, saying she
was merely experiencing double vision from her head
injury.

But Emily knew it wasn't just double vision. Something terrible had happened that day. And not just to
her.

Ever since the accident, her kind, gentle, loving
mother had changed into a stranger Emily no longer
knew.

At first, she'd thought the drastic change in her
mother was a result of Meredith's injuries in the accident. Emily had waited and waited, expecting the
cold, distant stranger who called herself her mother
to disappear, and her real mother to return.

It had never happened.

Words couldn't begin to describe the loss she'd
felt, still felt every single day. She'd loved her
mother, depended on her and now…

Emily sighed, checking the alarm box on the house
and wondering why the alarm was turned off. Her

parents always set the alarm before going out for the evening.

Now Emily wasn't certain she even knew or liked the woman who called herself her mother.

It was a loss she felt all the way to her soul. She couldn't talk to her dad about it, knowing that, he, too, sensed a change in her mom. She didn't want to upset him, didn't want him to know how deeply troubled she was by her mother's behavior.

With no one else to confide in, Emily had found herself confiding in her cousin Liza. At twenty, she was a few years younger than her cousin, who had the voice of an angel and a face to match.

Growing up, they'd become very close, and in some ways Liza had become a sister to her.

Liza completely understood Emily's confusion and fears about her mother. Liza's own mother was a cold, calculating, workaholic attorney who'd had little time for her, until she'd discovered Liza's beautiful singing voice.

Then Cynthia Turner Colton had become relentless in her pursuit to have Liza become a singing star. Liza's childhood had been reduced to lessons, practicing and performances, until the poor girl was so weary, all she wanted was some peace and quiet away from her controlling, demanding mother.

It was natural she gravitated toward the Colton house, and the warm, relaxed family atmosphere. Anxious to escape her own unhappy home, Liza spent as much time as possible at their house and had enjoyed a close, loving relationship with her Aunt Meredith, who had become like a surrogate mom to her.

It was a relationship that had also changed after the

accident. Now Meredith was cold and distant, with little time or patience for Liza. It was as if their past relationship had never happened.

It pained and worried both girls, so much so that they'd talked about it at length, confiding in each other their fears. The more bizarre Meredith's behavior became, the more alarmed the girls were.

So much so that Emily had recently confessed that she wondered if Meredith was really her mother.

It was as if her real mother had been stolen, and this cold, cruel stranger had taken her place.

The mere thought seemed ridiculous, outrageous, but it was the only explanation Emily could find to explain her adoptive mother's abrupt change in personality.

She no longer could even think of her as her mother, but Meredith.

With a sigh, Emily fumbled with her key, shivering in the darkness as the wind blew in from the coastline, chilling her.

She glanced up. The entire house was dark, even the light in her dad's first-floor study, which meant everyone was still out for the evening.

She unlocked the door and slipped inside, savoring the peace and quiet. Peace and quiet had become rare commodities when her mother was around.

Her dad had been seeing some old friends this evening, and her mother, well, who knew where her mother was for the evening; they rarely did. She came and went as she pleased, never bothering to tell anyone of her whereabouts.

Emily hated to admit she was relieved. She'd been far too upset all evening to have another confrontation with her mother over some perceived or imagined infraction.

All day and into the evening she'd had this terrible…premonition that something was horribly, terribly wrong. She'd tried to shake it off, telling herself she was merely being foolish. So she'd gone to dinner with some friends from school, and then to the movies, but still, the feeling hadn't left her.

After quietly shutting and locking the front door behind her, Emily rested her head against the cool wood, wishing things were different, wishing she had her once-happy life back.

Wishing she had her mother back.

Sadness engulfed her and she felt the sting of tears. She hadn't realized just how much she'd loved her mother until this had happened. Hadn't realized how much she'd depended on her mother until the accident.

Although she loved her father with a fierceness she couldn't even begin to put into words, it was her mother who had drawn her out of her shell with her loving kindness.

She'd been so young when she'd come to the Coltons, so young, and so frightened. Meredith was truly the only mother she knew. It was only through her unfailing love that Emily finally gained the confidence, the security to feel as if she was worthy of love, worthy of a family.

And then she'd blossomed. Confidence grew along with the love and devotion she'd had to her mother for making it all possible, for giving her the family, the love, the one place in the world she belonged.

But that was a long time ago, Emily thought with

a sigh, as she drew herself upward and made her way upstairs in the dark.

Her tennis shoes made no sound on the carpeted stairs.

For a moment she paused at the top of the stairs, grateful Meredith's bedroom was in the south wing, on the other side of the house.

Just being near Meredith now made her uncomfortable. She hoped to be in bed, sound asleep before the woman even came home.

At the top of the stairs, Emily frowned, wondering why her bedroom door was partially closed. Inez, their housekeeper, never closed their bedroom doors. In fact, the only time the bedroom doors were closed was when they were sleeping. In fact, that was how her dad knew when everyone was in for the night. It was his own version of a bed-check, one they'd all found amusing growing up.

Suddenly feeling that unease again, Emily paused.

It was so odd to have her bedroom door half-closed, like a puzzle piece that had been fit into the wrong place. Something so obvious, it would immediately garner attention.

Shaking, Emily quietly crept toward the door, glancing down the hallway. In the darkness, the silence seemed to echo loudly. For the first time in her life she was afraid in the big, sprawling house she had lived in as long as she could remember.

With trembling hands, she slowly pressed her fingertips against her bedroom door, opening it just enough so that she could see into the whole room. The open door hid her profile as her gaze scanned the darkened room.

Shafts of the moonlight filtered in through the draperies. But one of the windows was open, letting the drapes float in the evening breeze. Her fingers clutching the door, she froze, and a scream died in her throat.

Silhouetted against the moon's light was a man—a stranger hiding behind the drapes, near her bed.

Her eyes widened and she took a quiet step backward, pressing her free hand to her mouth to stifle a scream. Narrowing her eyes in the darkness, she felt her heart begin to hammer loudly in her chest, echoing in her ears, nearly deafening her.

It looked like he was holding—

"Oh God." The word came out an agonized whisper as fear and terror clutched her heart, nearly paralyzing her.

The man was holding a knife.

For years, because of her parents' position, because of their prominence in the community, all of the children had known they could become targets of some lunatic, for money, for fame, for glory, for whatever misguided notion such people had.

She'd never taken such a threat seriously before. Who on earth would want to hurt any of them? More importantly who would want to hurt *her?* And why? The thoughts came quickly, fragmented like a kaleidoscope, one tumbling over the other.

She was all alone in the house.

She had to get out!

Weak with fear, her knees nearly buckled as she whirled and rushed back down the stairs, almost stumbling on the last one. She grabbed the banister to catch herself, and a sob escaped her as she rushed toward the front door. The front door she had so carefully just locked.

Her hands were damp, shaking so badly, she couldn't get a grasp on the lock. The keys she still held clutched in her trembling hands slipped out, clattering to the marble floor.

She heard a noise behind her and turned. The man, his face clearly visible now, stood in her open bedroom doorway—with the knife.

He'd seen her!

She didn't bother to stop to pick up her keys. With an anguished cry, Emily flipped the lock, yanked open the door and bolted down the front steps, taking them two at a time, missing the last few and landing hard on her knees in the damp grass. The fall jolted her, nearly knocking the wind out of her.

Sobbing now, Emily looked around. She could hardly see through her tears. Other than the moonlight, it was pitch black. The only sound was the whispering of the wind echoing eerily in the darkness.

Shivering violently, from fear, from the chilly night, Emily swiped a hand across her eyes to clear her vision, trying to think.

She was alone.

With a madman.

She scrambled to her feet, pressing a hand to her pounding heart, ordering herself to move.

When she glanced back and saw him silhouetted now in the doorway, she nearly screamed. But screaming would do no good. No one would hear her. The ranch hands that worked on the estate were housed almost a mile away. Screaming would do little but alert the madman to her whereabouts.

Gasping, Emily raced around the north side of the house, past the sprawling kitchen, and the elegant dining room where they'd once shared so many wonderful holiday meals.

She had to hide.

She couldn't let him find her.

Her mind seemed immobilized; she kept moving, forcing herself to think. She tore around the back corner of the house, quickly glancing at the steps leading from the back of the house to the beach.

There was nowhere to hide.

She was out in the open, clearly visible, trapped between the ocean and the house.

And then it hit her.

The alcove.

About a hundred yards from the beach steps, the little alcove had been her and Liza's secret hiding place when they were children.

Their very own version of a playhouse, hidden from view and from the family. She and Liza had spent hours and hours in there, giggling, laughing, playing.

With another frantic glance behind her, Emily darted across the sand, her tennis shoes digging into the shifting granules, slowing her down, as her eyes adjusted to the darkness, searching out the small, almost hidden entrance.

Another noise behind her had her breath pumping out of her like a missing steam engine.

He was coming for her.

Her side ached from running, her knees were skinned from her fall, but she knew she couldn't stop.

She couldn't stop, couldn't let him find her.

"Dear God, help me," she sobbed. "Please, help me!"

She stumbled across the sand, found the darkened alcove entrance, realizing someone would miss it unless they knew it was there, knew where to look. Holding her breath, she slipped inside.

Pressing a hand to her heart, Emily crouched low to the sandy ground, pressing herself flat against the wall to conceal even her shadow.

With a deep, shaky breath, Emily covered her mouth with her hand and softly sobbed out a prayer. "Oh, Mom, help me. Where are you?"

Jackson, Mississippi

The nightmare woke her up.

She'd heard the child calling for her, calling for help. Heard the child, now a young woman, screaming in fear, terror.

"Mom, help me. Where are you?"

Gasping for air, Louise Smith bolted upright in bed, trying to claw her way out of the fog of terror swirling around her.

Her heart was pounding so loudly she could hear it thundering in her ears.

Her child was in danger.

In the darkness, the entire world seemed to be closing in on her, making her feel as if she were suffocating.

Ripping at the collar of her cotton nightgown, she tore it as she tried to drag air into her starving lungs.

Sweat pooled on her forehead, above her lip, between her breasts. She could hear the harsh, jerky sound of her own breathing as she fought for air.

The pain in her head, the blinding headache that always followed these nightmares, crept into her consciousness. The incessant pounding had her moaning softly.

Dear God, it was happening again. The dream. The little girl—*her* little girl, now a grown woman—was in danger, calling for her, begging her to help her, reaching out for her, needing her.

And she was powerless to do anything but watch in agony as her daughter helplessly fought off the evil surrounding her.

Louise shuddered in the darkness. The dream was so vivid, so real it replayed over and over in her mind like a broken record, torturing her.

She shook her head. She'd been having the same dream, seeing the same child for years, years that she'd been tormented by loneliness, by a loss so profound it was as if she had suffered a death.

Louise closed her eyes for a brief moment, and she could actually see the girl as clearly as if she'd been standing in front of her.

She was a small, frail child with a mop of curly red hair and an infectious smile. There was love and adoration radiating from the girl, and something else, a bond. The bond that only grew between mother and child.

The feeling was so strong, the vision so real, Louise shuddered in the darkness again, pressing a hand to her pounding forehead, then to her eyes to try to block out the vision.

The girl was now grown, a young woman, and she was in some kind of danger.

Louise knew it as sure as she knew that she was

lying in her own bedroom, in her own tidy little house.

Shuddering in the darkness, Louise blindly reached for the bottle of prescription medicine her therapist had prescribed to help ease the awful headaches, headaches that only came when she had these recurring nightmares.

Fumbling, she tried to snap off the bottle cap. It took all her energy to concentrate on the bottle, and not on the terror that gripped and controlled her body.

Her child was in danger.

No matter what anyone said, no matter what her therapist said, she knew she wasn't crazy. These dreams were too vivid, too real, the memories too strong.

"Mom, help me. Where are you?"

The cap to the bottle popped off, rolling to the floor. With shaking hands, Louise poured out a handful of little white pills, gulping one down dry. The rest she simply let slide out of her hand.

Closing her eyes, she held her trembling hands to her face, trying to regulate her breathing the way she'd been instructed. It took an intense amount of energy to ignore the incessant clamoring of her heart, the panicked, irrational fear.

Each moment seemed like an eternity as she tried to will the terror of her dream away.

Evil.

So much evil surrounding her child.

And she was powerless to help. She was impotent in the face of all that evil and terror.

Carefully, Louise concentrated on drawing air into her aching lungs, slowly, deeply, fighting back the lightheadedness the headache and nightmares left behind, waiting for the panic and terror to slowly subside.

Drenched with sweat, she battled the nausea that always followed the most severe nightmares.

"Mommy. Help me."

Louise blinked, trying to clear her clouded vision and focus on something—anything—other than herself and the feelings of helplessness, of fear that gripped her.

Bile rose in her throat. She swallowed convulsively several times. A sense of dread coupled with distaste settled in the pit of her stomach. Whatever was in her stomach didn't plan on being there much longer.

Pushing back the tumbled covers, she stumbled from the bed, praying her legs would hold her up.

Barefoot, she crept into the bathroom, clutching one hand to her mouth, one to her roiling stomach as she leaned over the bowl, unable to stop her body's violent physical protests.

By the time her stomach was emptied, the terror had nearly passed and her heartbeat and breathing were almost back to normal.

Still shaking, she turned on the cold water, cupped a handful to rinse her sour mouth, then grabbed a washcloth to bathe her face.

She caught a glimpse of herself in the mirror and almost didn't recognize the reflection staring back at her. Her nightgown was ripped; her short cap of golden brown hair now streaked with gray, was disheveled and her once sparkling brown eyes were ringed by shadows and looked dull and lifeless.

She stared at her reflection, wondering.

Who was she?

Louise Smith was a name she had taken after she'd been released from the institution. When she'd left, she had no memory of her past, no memory of who she had been or what she had done. It was only through the doctors that she'd learned of her painful past.

Shaking her head, Louise rubbed her hands over her face again. She couldn't bear the thought of what the doctors had told her she had done, been. So she'd taken a new name, started a new life.

But for years she had a feeling, a strong feeling that she'd had a child—children—a husband, someone who had been her other half.

But it wasn't who the doctors told her she was.

Why couldn't she remember?

Why couldn't she forget?

She may not have had any memories to recall, but she had something far stronger and more important: a feeling in her heart.

The bond she felt, the sense of deep loss she felt for her child—the little freckle-faced child with the mop of red hair had never dimmed—never went away. It was as if they were somehow still connected by love.

Louise turned away from her reflection, wiping down her face and neck with the cool rag.

She longed for a shower. Something to wash away the memories of the terror, the feelings of evil so she'd feel clean once again, but she didn't have enough energy left to even lift her arm to turn on the water. It would have to wait.

Stumbling back to her room, she began to shiver

uncontrollably. Grabbing the comforter from the bottom of the bed, she wrapped it tightly around her panic-racked body, then climbed back into bed.

Her hands were still trembling as she reached up to turn on the bedside lamp. Soft light flooded the small, cozy room and she took a slow, deep breath, looking at the spilled bottle of pills on the floor, wondering for a moment how they had gotten there.

She tugged the comforter up higher, then glanced toward her bedroom window that overlooked her beautiful garden.

There would be no more sleep for her tonight. She couldn't risk it, for she knew the moment she closed her eyes, she'd see the child again, her daughter, and the terror, the fear, the panic of helplessness would return.

So she'd simply wait for dawn to creep over the horizon. Wait and worry and pray that one day she'd remember who she really was, where her daughter was.

Pray that somehow, some way her child, her daughter, would be safe.

At least for this night.

Five

___

San Diego

Faith had been avoiding him for days.

Ali stood in the doorway of the sprawling room that held the entire systems operations for El-Etra Investments, quietly watching Faith, whose back was to him.

He glanced around the unfamiliar room, at a loss to understand what all the humming machines were. He shifted his attention back to Faith, absently loosening his tie against the warmth in the room.

Down here, in the bowels of the basement, even in the coolness of the late afternoon, it was warmer than the rest of the building. He'd talk to his building manager about it; there was no need for anyone to be uncomfortable while they worked.

"Faith?" He stepped into the room, amazed at her concentration. If she realized he was there, she gave no sign of it. Her eyes were focused on the computer screen in front of her, while her fingers flew over the keyboard.

Her shoulders were hunched forward, and he could see the line of tension in her back.

Quietly, he watched her for a moment, stunned anew at the impact she'd had on him. In spite of his hectic schedule, and the fact that he had not seen her in days, he found himself thinking of her several times during the day, or even in the darkness of the night.

Or he'd remember something she'd said, and find himself laughing out loud at the oddest moments. It happened just this morning during a meeting, causing him not just a little embarrassment, but some very strange looks indeed.

She was a most unusual woman, he decided, not his normal type, but a fascinating woman no less.

But judging from their last rather contentious encounter, her declaration that he would never have her, and the fact that he hadn't laid eyes on her in several days, apparently she had other ideas.

He walked farther into the room, stopping nearly beside her, but still she didn't even glance at him.

"Faith?" Smiling, he reached out and skimmed a finger down one errant curl, startling her.

She jumped in her chair, her eyes narrowing, then finally focusing on him.

"Ali." Faith shook her head, startled at his closeness, and the fact that he'd touched her.

She should have known he was in the room. Something in the air had changed, shifted with his presence. She'd felt it but had chosen to ignore it to concentrate on her work.

"You have been avoiding me," he accused with a smile, hitching one hip to the corner of the desk.

"No," she lied, turning back to the computer. "I've been doing what you're paying me to do. Working."

"Ah yes, working. I believe I've heard of that word." She glanced up just in time to see the amusement in his eyes, and realized he was teasing her.

She ordered her shoulders and hands to relax. They'd tightened up the moment she realized he was near.

He reached over and picked up her soft drink, taking a sip. Instantly, he made a face. "This is disgustingly warm."

"True, but I don't have time to go running around to get another."

All she had to do was complete the hook-up to the new server, and then she'd be halfway home, at least for this job. The balance of the job would take a few days, and she planned to let one of her other consultants handle it. She had no wish or desire to be this close to Ali on a day-to-day basis.

She couldn't trust him.

More importantly, she couldn't trust *herself*. Not after the other night at the black-tie gala. She knew it, and she intended to do something about it, which was why she'd been working at such a feverish pace, so she could let someone else complete the job. She had to avoid Ali at all costs.

She'd done a good job thus far—until about three

minutes ago when he'd sailed into the room, bringing his masculine intensity with him, causing her brains to scramble and her temperature to rise.

"What are you doing down here? Besides mooching my soda." She took her glass from him, took a sip, then realized he was right, it was disgustingly warm.

"Actually, I came to see if you'd deliberately been avoiding me, or if perhaps you'd been abducted by aliens."

Still trying to concentrate, she glanced away from the monitor and up at him with an annoyed frown. "What?"

"Aliens," he repeated, realizing she was somewhere else, thinking of something else. He admired that kind of intense concentration and dedication, but he did wish she wasn't quite so surly all the time.

It was the first time in his life a woman had actually, deliberately ignored or avoided him. It wasn't just a challenge he couldn't resist, but something more, something about Faith Martin had stirred him in a way other women had not.

In spite of his fears about his own reaction to her, he was also a man, with a healthy male ego. He found Faith not just a challenge, but an intriguing puzzle he wanted to solve.

"What about aliens?" she asked with a shake of her head, finally registering his words. "And why are you bothering me?" she demanded, not wanting to encourage him to stay.

She was hot, tired and incredibly irritable. She'd skipped breakfast and lunch, and now had a splitting headache. She really was not in the mood for jokes or flirtatious banter. "I'm busy."

Shaking his head, Ali laughed. All of his other employees nearly shook in their shoes when they saw him; she merely snarled at him.

"Yes, I can see that you're busy," he said, glancing over her shoulder to see what she was doing. He didn't have a clue. "And in a good mood again, I see."

Faith rubbed her throbbing temple, then blew out a breath. His presence was only adding to her irritability. She may have been deliberately avoiding him, but that hadn't meant she hadn't seen him.

In this morning's paper, in the middle of the society pages, there he was, arm around another long, leggy blonde.

From the dizzying array of pictures so far this week, Ali apparently hadn't been too bothered by her refusal.

In spite of Kadid's enlightenment, Ali's behavior served to confirm her worst suspicions about him and his character. His parents might be fixing him up, but he was the one playing musical chairs with all of these women. He didn't have to go out with a different one every night. Didn't he ever hear of staying home?

She wondered how many women's hearts Ali had broken with his careless disregard. She'd watched her own father use and discard women like burned-out matches. Scorch one, then move on to the next without further thought of their feelings. Or anyone else's but his own.

"So then what do you want?" she demanded, letting her annoyance slip into her voice.

"I told you, I came to see if you've deliberately been avoiding me," he said with careful patience.

"Don't be ridiculous," she lied.

"Faith?" He touched a tendril of hair again, a slight frown marring his brow. Instinctively, she jerked back at his touch, remembering what that touch could do to her, reduce her to.

"What?" She rubbed her forehead, wishing that he didn't irritate her so, but that irritation was merely her own frustration and annoyance at her own reactions to him.

She should be able to control her body, shouldn't have it doing traitorous things just because he was near. It felt like a betrayal on the most basic level and she wasn't sure how to deal with it.

She glanced up at him and saw the heat of emotion in his eyes. Unable to determine exactly what that emotion was, she sighed. He was still the boss, and she should at least make an attempt to be civil, if for no other reason than to keep things on a professional level. "Why on earth would you think I was avoid—"

"We had an appointment over an hour ago," Ali said quietly, patiently, lifting the cuff of his shirt to show her his watch. It was almost seven in the evening.

Her eyes widened and she jumped to her feet. "Good Lord, I completely forgot the time." Frustrated, she pushed her hair off her face. "I'm sorry." Shaking her head, she blew out another frustrated breath. "I wasn't avoiding you or trying to be rude.

Honest.'' At least it was the truth—this time. She *had* forgotten their appointment. "I got so caught up in what I was doing, I completely lost all track of time."

There was a scattering of notes across the table, notes she'd prepared earlier this morning for their meeting so she could give him a status report on his system.

Flustered now, she began scooping them up, trying to put them in some semblance of order.

"Relax," he said quietly, getting to his feet. She was unaccountably rattled and he didn't understand why. It aroused a whole host of feelings in him.

At the moment, she didn't look strong and capable, but merely frazzled, fragile and oddly vulnerable. Something he had not imagined in the very capable Faith.

It brought out every protective male instinct in his body, causing something inside to soften.

"Calm down, Faith, it's not that big a deal. I was tied up in an investors' meeting across town and just got back a few moments ago myself." He laid a hand on her shoulder to calm her.

Her tense, tired body reacted instantly to his touch. She froze, and then the heat rushing through her seemed to melt everything inside, causing her words, her thoughts to scatter.

"I guess I just got so involved…I was so engrossed…I didn't realize how late it was."

"It's not a problem, no harm done," he all but crooned as the hand on her shoulder started to knead her tense muscles and Faith sighed in spite of herself.

She hated to admit it, but her muscles were screaming with strain and fatigue. And her stomach ached from hunger. His touch seemed to arouse every single sore nerve ending, making them squeal in alarm, but she was too tired to hear them.

"Turn around," he said quietly, and with a weary sigh, she did as she was told, turning her back to him.

His hands were large, warm, and yet incredibly gentle as he massaged her tight shoulders, gently kneading the pressure points until she felt relaxation slowly creep over her.

"You have been working too hard," he admonished, his breath, his words, like a soft, gentle caress against the exposed skin on her neck.

Vividly aware of his touch, of his body so close to hers, Faith felt as if a charge of electricity sparked between them, connecting them with the kind of heat that could scorch them both.

Scorches left scars, she reminded herself.

She tensed up, then tried to pull away, suddenly frightened, wondering how he could cause her to stop thinking simply by touching her.

"Faith, this will do no good if you continue to tense up. Please just let yourself go for a moment." His hands worked their magic against the tightness that gripped her whole body. "Just relax."

She could feel the tension slowly drain from her as he moved his hands over her skin and her light cotton T-shirt.

A shiver raced over her as her body reacted. Her breasts grew heavy, the nipples taut. She had to concentrate to get breath in and out of her lungs.

"Your body is protesting all the tension you've been carrying around. Such stress is not good for you.'' He inhaled deeply of her hair, the scent like a soothing balm to his frustrated body.

He continued to knead, to massage, letting the pads of his fingers work their magic.

Letting her eyes slide closed, Faith wanted to purr in ecstasy, certain nothing had ever felt so wonderful.

''And you have a headache as well,'' he commented, sliding his fingers up the back of her neck to massage the tightened muscles where the headache seemed to have clustered.

With each stroke, the throbbing seemed to ease, doing what several doses of aspirin had failed to do.

''You've obviously missed your calling,'' she murmured.

''My calling?'' he asked in confusion.

She sighed in pleasure again, allowing herself, *ordering* herself to relax and enjoy this few moments of pleasure.

''Yes, you should have been a masseur. You have great hands.''

''Thank you. I shall ask Kadid to put that on my resume.''

Faith laughed, realizing he had a dry, wicked sense of humor, something she found incredibly appealing when she wasn't totally annoyed at the man. ''Well, that ought to impress all your clients.''

He chuckled, his fingers still moving upward to release her hair from its constraints. It fell free to her shoulders, and as his fingers combed through the beautiful, fiery strands, he remembered how she'd looked the other night, with her hair framing her face, emphasizing the delicacy of her features.

His fingers moved to her scalp, circling, rubbing,

pressing until she wanted nothing more than to lean back against him and abandon her aching, tired body to his expert touch.

''Well, I'm pleased that something about me actually pleases you.'' Although he would like to please her in other ways, sensual ways. He was a normal, healthy man, and she was a normal, healthy, if a bit surly, woman. She was so surprisingly different and real, so genuine in a way he had almost stopped believing women could be.

She responded to his touch with abandon, not bothering to hide her pleasure just as she had the other night when she was in his arms.

It was rare for a woman to relish the simplest of touches. It made him curious how she would respond to other, more intimate touches.

He knew, he realized, knew instinctively. All he had to do was remember the heat, the passion, the fire that she'd given to him from just one kiss.

The thought brought an instant stirring to his blood. He wanted her in his arms again, wanted to taste her, to touch her, to know her intimately in the way a man could only really know a woman.

Knowing he could not sustain such thoughts without embarrassing himself, he ordered his hands to move to her temples, massaging in a gentle circular motion.

''Good Lord, this is wonderful.'' With a moan, Faith gave in and closed her eyes. ''Almost decadent.''

The feel of her under his hands and her unbridled response was bringing incredible pleasure. Before he was overwhelmed, he deliberately shifted his thoughts.

"Have you eaten today?" he asked quietly.

"Two candy bars and a bag of chips." Her voice sounded more like a purr.

"You may be very good at what you do, Faith Martin," he said quietly, "but I'm afraid you're not so good at taking care of yourself."

His sweet breath warmed her neck, causing goose bumps to rise and her heart to thud so loudly she feared he might hear it. She had to swallow hard before she spoke because her mouth had gone dry.

"I consider candy and chips two of the basic food groups."

"And then of course there is your favorite cola." He glanced down at the soggy cup that held the now-warm liquid.

"That's merely fuel to keep me going." Almost totally relaxed now, Faith rolled her shoulders, bringing her body close enough to bump against the firm hardness of his. His fingers unconsciously tightened on her shoulders, causing her to freeze.

From shoulder to hip they were touching, pressed against each other, her back against his chest, heat flowing from one to the other.

Ali heard her breath catch, and felt the responding blood pool in his gut, then shift painfully lower. He almost groaned.

Stunned anew, Faith froze, vividly aware that she was pressed against the long, hard length of him, much the same way she'd been the other night.

She'd tried to forget what had happened that night, tried to pretend it didn't happen.

But she couldn't forget the way his touch made her feel, couldn't forget the feel of his lips on hers. Or the way her body had responded.

Ordering herself to think, she tried to take a step forward, to put some space between them, to break the connection between them, but his hands held her gently, but firmly.

"You are getting all tense again," he admonished. "I promise I won't bite." He could not bear to release her yet, yet he felt unable to explain this unaccountable need to touch her.

He turned her slowly to face him, smiling at the soft look on her face. Her eyes were a bit dreamy, sparkling like fine emeralds.

Her hair, that fiery tangle of red and gold that fell just to her shoulders, framed her face like a halo, emphasizing her fragile ivory complexion. Her cheeks now held a hint of color, but it only added to her appeal.

Looking at him as if in a trance, Faith realized he might not bite but he had enough experience with women to know the effect he was having on her. She was not immune to men; she simply chose to keep them at bay out of necessity. The necessity of self-protection.

Wanting to get things back on a more professional level, she stepped away from him.

"Thanks for the massage," she said lightly, gathering her hair in her hands to pull it back up. She felt far too defenseless with her hair down. "My headache's almost gone." He laid a hand on hers, stopping her from pulling her hair up.

"Don't," he said quietly. "Your hair is beautiful.

Magnificent.'' With her hair down, she looked soft, beautiful and incredibly bewitching. How could any man resist?

"Did you know in my country that a woman's hair is her glory?" His gaze went over her hair, pleased. "It is a sign of beauty. You should wear your hair down more often. It's beautiful."

"Well then, I guess it's a good thing I don't live in your country," she murmured, suddenly feeling self-conscious. "Because I can't wear my hair down when I work. It might get caught in something." She grabbed a rubber band from the desk and caught her hair up in it. Her hands were trembling so much she had to do it twice.

He was still too close, far too close. She needed to put some distance between them so she could regain her composure.

"Pity," he said with a soft smile.

She began gathering up her notes. "Look, if it's not too late, we can still have our meeting. Just give me a few minutes to get my stuff together."

And to get back some composure. She was babbling like a schoolgirl, trying to fill the awkward silence with words that she wasn't certain even made sense.

She didn't like feeling off balance, didn't like feeling like she'd lost control. When had it shifted from her to him?

The moment he touched her, she realized, trying to understand the power he had over her.

"You're tired, Faith. I think we should wait until morning. Have dinner with me instead."

His request took her by surprise and she glanced up at him warily. "No, I'm sorry, I can't."

"Can't. Or won't?" He watched her carefully.

Faith shrugged, realizing she was treading on dangerous ground. She had to be careful; he was still the boss, and she didn't want to do anything else to further jeopardize this job. "Doesn't matter, really, the result is the same."

"Oh, but it does matter, Faith," he retorted. "To me. *Can't* means you have a prior commitment. *Won't* means you don't care to spend the time with me, to share a meal with me."

"Ali, look." Hesitating, she pushed a few hairs off her cheek. "I'm sure you're a very nice person—"

"You're lying again, Faith," he said softly, letting a small smile curve his mouth. "I do not think you are sure of any such thing." It bothered him, he realized, that she still thought so poorly of him.

Determined to tackle the problem head-on, Faith met his gaze. "I make it a practice never to get involved with anyone I work with."

There, it was out on the table. She was not interested in becoming one of his revolving playmates.

"Involved?" One brow rose and he looked at her thoughtfully. "I didn't realize dinner was that complicated."

"It's usually not," she admitted, realizing the way he'd phrased her words back to her made her feel unaccountably foolish.

"But in my case it is?"

"Could be." Tightening her fingers on her notes, Faith held his gaze, refusing to back down. She wasn't about to admit what the man's presence did to her. To do so would only feed his enormous ego.

"I just think it's best if we not...socialize," she said with a careless shrug of her slender shoulders. "It can lead to...complications." It wasn't the right word, but it would do for the moment.

"Socialize?" One brow rose. "I wasn't aware that I was asking you to socialize. I was merely suggesting we continue our business meeting over dinner. You obviously have not eaten, and neither have I, and quite frankly, I've had a very long day and am quite hungry." His smile was slow. "My suggestion was nothing more than that."

He was not accustomed to lying and found the words rang hollowly. But he knew if he admitted the truth, that he just wanted to spend time with her, she'd never agree to have dinner with him.

"And the only complication I can foresee, Faith, is what you would prefer to eat."

Concerned now that perhaps she had misinterpreted his actions, Faith felt her face grow warm as she searched his gaze. He looked as innocent as a new-born babe, making her wonder if perhaps she *had* misunderstood his intentions.

"You are hungry, yes?" he prodded.

Feeling trapped, she nodded dully.

"Good." His smile flashed brilliantly. "So we will continue our meeting over dinner. You can bring me up to date on the system, and I can tell you about my conversation with Abner Josslyn this afternoon. It will save time, and we can satisfy our appetites. It is— what do you call it—multi-tasking, I believe?"

"You talked to Abner Josslyn this afternoon?"

Anxious, she took a step forward, remembering his promise to speak to Mr. Josslyn about her.

"Yes, as a matter of fact I did." He slipped his hands in his pockets to prevent himself from touching her again. He wanted to lay a hand to her cheek, to soothe the worry, the tension he saw there. "It was a very pleasant and profitable conversation as well. We can discuss it at length at dinner." He turned to leave. "Meet me at the Coronado, it's in the lobby of the Hotel—"

"I know where it is," she snapped, slightly offended by his arrogant tone. "I'm not a complete social moron."

He merely smiled, refusing to be baited. "Fine." He glanced at his watch. "Shall we say thirty minutes, then? I need to make a quick call first."

"Fine." Thirty minutes should just give her enough time to gather her composure and shore up her defenses.

"I'll see you then." Ali turned and left her standing there, notes clutched in her hands, wondering how she was supposed to swallow a single bite of food with the man sitting next to her.

"The Coronado," Faith muttered miserably. Couldn't he have picked a less intimidating spot?

The four-star hotel that housed the Coronado restaurant sat high atop a bluff, overlooking the beautiful grounds and gardens of the magnificent old-world hotel that had been built in the early twenties and restored to all its original glory.

Private bungalows were discreetly tucked around the grounds, which meandered through the entire acreage, past the two kidney-shaped pools, and the spas.

The restaurant itself was just as old, just as impressive and had also been totally restored to its heyday complete with impeccable service and outstanding food.

The antiques that adorned every nook and cranny of the Coronado were rumored to be authentic and worth a small fortune.

It figured, Faith thought with a scowl. Elegant, intimate, and definitely more than a bit romantic with its candle-lit tables, and soft harp music floating quietly through the room.

This was definitely *not* the kind of restaurant in which she would normally envision conducting business. At least not her business.

She'd have much preferred somewhere where she could have a cheeseburger, fries and a cola, and relax in her T-shirt and jeans.

She started to laugh, wondering exactly how the arrogant Sheik Ali El-Etra was going to react when the Coronado's maître d' took one look at her absolutely inappropriate attire and promptly and firmly tossed her raggedy butt out?

Six

"**I** half-expected the maître d' to toss me out on my butt," Faith admitted with a laugh as she sipped the ice-cold soda Ali had graciously ordered before she'd arrived.

Muted conversation and the soft strings of a harp wafted softly through the air.

"Toss you out?" he repeated with an amused lift of his brow. "And why on earth would you assume such a ridiculous thing?"

Faith laughed, carefully setting her glass down on the tablecloth. It was the first time she could ever remember drinking cola out of Baccarat crystal. "Because I'm not exactly dressed for an elegant dinner in a place like this."

"On the contrary, Faith, you look lovely." He gave her hand a reassuring pat, not daring to admit that he had already discussed this rather delicate situation with the staff of the restaurant.

Although Charles, the maître d', was widely known for enforcing the dress code, not even he would dare insult one of Sheik El-Etra's guests.

"Well, thanks," she said, glancing around the dining room.

The floor-to-ceiling windows glistened against the night's darkness, reflecting the twinkling of the soft candles inside and the magnificent sprawl of stars outside.

Each table was covered in a snowy white linen tablecloth edged in Battenburg lace. The supple red leather booths constructed in a half circle seemed to caress each one of the patrons, providing an intimate alcove of privacy. Their corner booth was set against one of the glass walls, allowing an unobstructed view of the bluffs below. Under other circumstances, she realized this could be an incredibly romantic setting for lovers. But this was a business dinner, and Ali was definitely not her lover.

Uncomfortable with her thoughts, Faith shifted in the booth. An ice bucket sat to the right of their booth, but instead of a cold bottle of expensive champagne, it held several bottles of cola, almost making Faith laugh again.

"Have you decided?" Ali asked politely, sipping his own mineral water.

"I haven't even looked at the menu." When she did, she tried not to gape at the prices. "You could feed a third-world country for what they're charging for one meal." She scowled. "I don't suppose they serve cheeseburgers?"

Ali almost choked on his drink. Convulsively, he swallowed several times before setting his glass down.

Not in memory had a woman ever worried or considered the price of *anything* when she was with him. It was, in spite of his shock, rather charming. He didn't know which amused him more—her concern over the prices, or her rather unusual dinner request.

"Cheeseburgers?" he repeated as if she'd just requested raw rats for dinner. "Why not allow me to order for us?"

Hesitant, Faith worried her lower lip, thinking about the tank of live lobsters she saw as she came in.

"Okay, but if it's going to be fish, nothing with eyes." She shifted. "I don't eat anything that can watch me while I'm eating it." The mere thought had her shuddering, making Ali laugh.

"I promise." He lifted his hand solemnly. "Nothing with eyes." He hesitated a moment. "Except potatoes. You do eat potatoes, don't you?" he asked with a lift of his brow.

She grinned. "Make it French fries and you've got a deal."

With a nod, Ali signaled for a waiter, then placed their order. Faith waited until he was finished before asking her question.

"Okay, so tell me about your conversation with Mr. Josslyn."

Thoughtfully, Ali fingered the rim of his glass. "Well, Abner only had a few minutes, so I suggested we get together for lunch next week."

"We?" Faith looked at him carefully. "Define 'we.'"

Ali laughed. Her mind was just one of her many assets. A refreshing change from the women he usually dined with. "I'd forgotten how perceptive you are." He sipped his drink, taking his time, glancing around.

Faith was antsy. She was dying to hear about his conversation with old man Josslyn, and he was drawing it out like it was a world secret.

"Ali?" she prompted, and he smiled slowly at her, pausing while the waiter set down their salads.

"Very well, I can see that you are impatient. I told Abner that I thought it would be a smart business move on his part to meet you." Ali shrugged, then picked up his fork and tasted his salad. "I suggested lunch next week when he returns from the East Coast. I told him by then you should have our system up and working again." He hesitated, his fork hovering over his plate. "You will have our system back up and working, won't you?"

"Of course."

She wasn't about to blow that bonus Ali had promised her. She had plans for it, big plans.

"Good, good." Ali nodded, then resumed eating. "Anyway, at lunch I can tell him the things you've done for El-Etra, and then perhaps you can discuss upgrading his entire computer system as well."

Faith frowned, picking at her salad, more interested in Ali's conversation than her food. "For which company?"

Abner Josslyn was the head of an international conglomerate of companies that did business around the world.

"All of them," Ali said with a smile, watching the excitement light Faith's eyes. It pleased him to make her happy, he realized.

She swallowed, then slowly set her fork down, not certain she'd heard him correctly. "*All* of them?"

Her head was suddenly spinning. The opportunity, the possibilities, and what this meeting could mean to her consulting firm if she landed the entire Josslyn conglomerate was staggering.

"I trust you are pleased?" Sipping his drink, Ali watched her.

"Pleased?" Faith fairly beamed at him. "I'd say that's the word for it. Not the right word, mind you. But it will do. For now." Thrilled, she couldn't resist leaning close and giving his hand an appreciative squeeze. "Ali, thank you. I can't tell you how much I appreciate your help."

He caught her hand in his, then raised it to his lips for a kiss, sending a ripple of awareness over her. They were sitting barely an inch apart, their hips touching, connecting them on a whole other level.

"But I have done nothing, Faith." With his gaze intent on hers, he kissed her hand again, enjoying the touch, the taste of her, the way her eyes darkened with each kiss. "This is all your work, your expertise." He shrugged, contenting himself with kissing her fingertips one by one. "You are the one who has made this possible." He smiled. "I merely am the facilitator, bringing two people together who need each other." His gaze caught hers and there was something dark and dangerous in his eyes. It made her shiver.

"And what else do you need, Faith?" His voice had dropped, it was low, husky and sent her heart fluttering.

"N-need?" She tried to laugh, but it came out a croak. "I really don't need anything."

She managed a smile and withdrew her hand, not comfortable with where this was going. Then she picked up her fork and pushed her salad around her plate some more.

"My life is pretty full," she said, rushing on, not certain she liked the timbre of his voice or the intent of his words. He'd managed to take a simple business conversation and turn it into something that sounded decidedly like a...seduction.

Remembering what had happened the other night, at the gala, Faith knew she was treading on dangerous ground. She didn't want to get into any type of personal conversation with him. She didn't think she could handle it, not knowing how the man affected her.

Good grief, all he had to do was look at her with those deep, mysterious eyes, or smile that sensuous smile and her knees were buckling. It was quite annoying, she decided, determined to keep things very businesslike.

"I have my business and it keeps me very busy. Then there's the managing and hiring of all my employees." She flashed him a shaky smile, talking a mile a minute. "You know how that can be. Employees can sometimes be like children. They squabble, they mark their territory. Sometimes I'm not sure if I'm running a business or a day care. But it keeps me very busy. My life is incredibly full. I really don't need or have time for much else.''

"But, Faith," he said carefully, "do you not find your life just a bit boring with only business to fill your time?''

"Boring?" She considered it for a moment. Lonely, perhaps, she thought silently. There were times she ached with loneliness. She spent so much time with machines that at times she longed to hear just another human voice.

But she wasn't about to admit such a thing to *him.*

Faith forced a laugh. "Boring is not a word that I encounter very often. There's always something interesting happening. Always some new snafu that takes me by surprise.'' She shrugged, realizing that talking about her business, something she knew was solid, was allowing her to relax a bit. "The world is moving so fast, and technology with it, that sometimes it's difficult to keep up. So I'm never bored.''

He was having trouble concentrating on her words when her delicate fragrance was playing havoc with his senses. "What about your social life, Faith? Surely you have time to socialize?''

"Nope.'' She shook her head and broke off a piece of crusty bread from the basket. "I'm not much into socializing.'' She shrugged, nibbled her bread. "Unless it's for business, like the other night, I'm not much for crowds or fancy get-togethers.''

"I see,'' he said thoughtfully, sipping his drink and watching her over his glass. "And what about men? Is there someone special in your life?''

How he'd managed to turn this from a business

discussion into a discussion of her love life was beyond her. He was quite smooth.

Hoping to ignore the question, Faith broke off another piece of bread, then glanced around the quiet, elegant room.

"Faith?" He took her hand again, caressing it, stroking his own fingers up and down hers in a way that heated her blood and sent it pulsing through her veins.

She inhaled a deep breath. Was someone siphoning the air? It was getting hard to breathe.

"No." She concentrated on blowing her breath out slowly. "There's no one special."

He looked pleased, but not surprised. "I see." With his gaze still intent on hers, he brought her hand to his lips once more, kissing it again, making her heart dance a wicked beat beneath her T-shirt.

Faith's eyes widened. "Uh, Ali?"

Embarrassed, she tried to tug her hand free as she watched a couple approach their table. He refused to relinquish her hand, kissing it once again.

"I'm very pleased to hear—"

"Ali." Faith's voice held a sense of urgency as she tried to tug her hand free once again. "I think we…we're about to have company." Her eyes widened in alarm as an elegant, well-dressed couple approached their booth.

The man was tall, dark and broad-shouldered; he glowed with vigor and vitality. Although thickening around the waist, he was impeccably attired. His profile was strong, sharp, and although his hair was short, and a deep, rich black, it was tinged with silver around the temples.

The resemblance to Ali was so strong, so striking, Faith knew instinctively it had to be his father. Why this alarmed her, she didn't know.

Her gaze shifted to the woman with him. She was not beautiful in the traditional sense, but she had a distinct air of elegance. Her features were an interesting, exotic mix of high cheekbones, small, upturned nose and the most beautiful near-black eyes Faith had ever seen. Her lips were delicately sculptured and painted a smart sleek red.

She was small and delicate, with dark hair swept into a fashionable style. Still model-slender, she wore an impeccable suit in a pale shade of ice-blue, complemented by matching jewels that sparkled at her ears and on her small, slender fingers.

Ali glanced behind him and released Faith's hand as a wide smile sheathed his face, softening it.

"Father." Ali's face lit up like a beacon, his gaze going from his father to his mother. Clearly he was both pleased and surprised.

Watching him, Faith was stunned by the transformation. It was like the day with Maureen Jourdan. Gone was the arrogant, aristocratic facade, replaced by a man of warmth and love. It was clear to see he adored his parents.

"Son." With a broad smile, Sheik Omar El-Etra laid a large, bronzed hand on his son's shoulder and gave it an affectionate squeeze.

Although dressed in a three-piece suit, he also wore a *kalfiylh*, the traditional loose head scarf that was held in place by decorative cords.

"Father." Smiling broadly, Ali openly embraced his father. "What a pleasant surprise." He patted his father's back affectionately. "It is so good to see you."

His father returned the hug, smiling at Faith over Ali's shoulder. "It is good to see you as well, my son."

Ali kissed his father's cheeks, then stepped out of his father's embrace and caught his mother up in a ferocious hug.

"Mom."

"My son." Tibi El-Etra laid loving hands to her son's cheeks, her eyes shining with pride. "We've missed you."

With a laugh of joy, Ali tightened his arms around his mother, nearly lifting her off the ground.

"And I have missed you." He swung her around in a circle, making her laugh before releasing her, and kissing her on each cheek as well, then dropping a protective arm around her slender shoulders.

The gesture was so loving, Faith couldn't help but stare, wondering if this was the same man she'd gotten to know the past week.

"It is so wonderful to see you," Ali glanced down at his mother. "You look as beautiful as ever."

"And you, my son, still know how to flatter."

Ali glanced at Faith, his face still sheathed in pleasure. "Please, forgive my manners. This is Faith Martin. Faith, this is my mother, Tibi El-Etra, and my father, Omar El-Etra."

Feeling a bit self-conscious since she'd been caught by Ali's parents having her fingers kissed, Faith felt her face grow warm as she started to stand to greet them.

"Sit, sit," his father admonished with a warm

smile, waving her back down into her seat. "Please, do not get up on our account." His glance was loving as he looked at his wife. "We are not a family who stands on ceremony."

Faith sat back down, watching them, trying not to feel envious. It was clear that this was a family in the true sense of the word. There was love, devotion and trust between them, radiating through the air, connecting them in a way she'd never known.

She glanced at Ali's father and saw the pride, the pleasure in his gaze as he looked at his wife and son, and felt a stab of pain deep in her heart.

"It's a pleasure to meet you both," she said, scooting over in the booth to make room for them.

"Please, join us?" Ali stepped aside to allow his mother to slide into the booth, carefully pulling the table out for her. Tibi slid in next to Faith, glancing at her warmly. Omar slid in next to his wife, draping an arm casually, affectionately around her shoulder.

"Have you had dinner yet?" Ali slid back into the booth next to Faith, much closer now that his parents had joined them. Their hips, their legs were touching, and Faith felt the heat of him warm her, startling her. "We've just ordered, but I'll be glad to—"

"We've eaten already." Tibi smiled across the table at her son. "We had a late lunch with the Coltons while they were in town."

"And how are they?" Ali asked politely.

"Fine. We gave them your love."

Tibi turned to Faith to include her in the conversation. "We came to California a few months ago to attend the birthday party of a very old and dear friend, Joe Colton."

"Yes, I know. Ali told me."

Tibi and her husband exchanged curious glances. "Do you know the Coltons?" Tibi's glance skimmed over Faith, then beamed with approval. The young woman was lovely. Although she wasn't anything like the young women Ali usually dated, there was something refreshingly innocent about her.

Tibi was instantly curious, and if the scene they'd witnessed as they approached—her son holding the young woman's hand—was any indication, there was more here than her son had let on.

Interesting, she decided, letting her gaze go from her son back to Faith.

"No, not really." Faith hesitated. "I've never actually met them, but I know of them." She took a deep breath, then met Tibi's interested gaze.

Faith rarely talked about her childhood with anyone. It was far too painful, but it would seem rude not to explain.

"I spent some time at the Hopechest Ranch when I was growing up." Her smile was shaky. "That's how I became aware of the Coltons and their generosity."

"Ah, I see." Tibi's smile warmed and she laid a hand over Faith's, realizing there was far more to this young woman than met the eye.

From her plain clothing it was obvious she was not one of the beautiful, wealthy, infinitely boring little socialites her son seemed to prefer.

Perhaps there was hope for her son and his future after all.

"I'm on the Board of the Hopechest Ranch," Tibi said, watching Faith carefully.

"It's a wonderful place," Faith admitted. "They do some incredible things for kids." If it wasn't for the ranch, she had no idea what would have become of her.

"Yes, they do," Tibi agreed. "I'm happy to hear that your experience there was pleasant."

"Yes, it was," Faith said, making Ali wonder about Faith's childhood.

He'd been listening intently, and now he wondered why Faith had grown up on a ranch for troubled children.

Oh, he knew the Hopechest Ranch didn't just take in troublemakers, but also children who had nowhere else to go, children whose families had been broken or separated for whatever reason.

He sincerely doubted that serious, sincere Faith had ever been in trouble. No, it had to be some other reason that had sent her to the ranch.

With his brows drawn together in concentration, he wondered about Faith, realizing in all this time he had never once asked Faith about her background, her family, her childhood.

Where were her parents, he wondered, feeling a bit of anger toward them. Why had they allowed their daughter to be raised by strangers?

It didn't make sense.

He glanced at his own parents, his eyes, his heart filled with love. He knew how difficult it had been for him to come to America, to be separated from them even for a brief time, but he always knew they were there for him, always knew he was part of a loving family and had their full support.

Apparently Faith had not had the benefit of a loving, supportive family. It touched something deep inside of him, and he found himself reaching for her hand under the table. For once, she didn't resist him.

"So, Ali." Omar turned to his son. "How was your evening with Clarissa?"

"Clarissa?" Ali frowned. Who on earth was Clarissa, he wondered, frantically trying to remember.

Tibi laughed, amused. "Clarissa, dear, the niece of Senator Bigelow, the beautiful young woman you escorted to the black-tie charity gala the other night?" She exchanged glances with her husband, and one dark brow arched upward. "Apparently the evening wasn't that memorable."

Clarissa?

Obviously that was the name of his date the night he'd rescued Faith from Aaron Josslyn.

All he remembered of that night was the way Faith looked. His gaze shifted to hers now and he felt a warmth unfold inside, remembering that night and how she'd looked and felt in his arms.

"Ali?" his mother prompted, her smile still amused. "Since you're apparently not interested in Clarissa, if you're not busy tomorrow evening, your father and I met a lovely young woman this evening. She's the daughter of a very old and dear friend of your father's. We thought perhaps—"

"Mother." Ali took a deep breath, then glanced at Faith. He couldn't bear the thought of spending any more of his evenings bored to tears with empty-headed women whose only interest was his bank account. Nor did he want to hurt his parents' feelings. "There's something you should know."

The tone of his voice had Tibi and Omar exchanging concerned glances.

"What is it, son?" Omar asked quietly, drawing his wife closer to provide unspoken support. "Is something wrong? Are you ill? In trouble?" Concern etched deeply into the creases of his face.

Ali shook his head. "No, Father. I'm sorry, I did not mean to alarm you. It's nothing like that." He hesitated, then glanced at Faith, tightening his hold on her hand and hoping she would understand what he was about to do. "I have something to tell you, something I hope will please you both." And stop their infernal matchmaking. "Faith and I...are engaged to be married."

Stunned speechless by Ali's announcement, Faith felt her mouth drop open as if it had come unhinged, and she gaped at him as if he'd just announced he was about to give birth to a baboon.

Engaged?

Engaged!

Was the man insane?

What on earth was he thinking?

Furious, she tried to snatch her hand free, the better to whack him—but he held on tight, refusing to relinquish her.

"What?" Tibi's smile went from Faith, back to Ali. "But when did this happen?" Overjoyed, and slightly overwhelmed, Tibi shook her head, trying to take it all in. This was her very wish, her every dream come true. "But...why did you not tell us?" Her hand went to her happily thudding heart. "How...how..." Shaking her head, she laughed again. "I have so many questions, but I am so happy

I don't think I can get them all out. When did you two meet? How did you two meet?" She laughed again, realizing the questions were pouring from her mouth.

Leaning back in the booth, Ali hung on to Faith's hand for dear life, praying she wouldn't give away his little fabrication.

"Faith and I met a while ago. And actually, it was Kadid who introduced us," Ali explained, earning a heated glare from Faith.

Was there no end to the man's lies?

While it was true that Kadid *had* introduced them on the day she'd stormed into Ali's office, it certainly was *not* the way Ali had made it seem to his parents.

"Ah, Kadid," his father said with an approving nod. "He is a most wise man and has been a loyal and valuable servant."

"But why did you not tell us?" Tibi asked, a hint of hurt in her voice.

"I apologize, Mother. It was certainly not intentional." Ali gave Faith a warm look. The look she gave him back should have had steam lifting from his skin. "But it happened very suddenly. Right, Faith dear?"

She managed to glare at him. "Yes, *dear*." Her teeth hurt from clenching them together. "Very suddenly." She glanced at his parents, then forced herself to smile. "So suddenly it even took me by surprise."

"I apologize, Father, but I'm sure you can understand." Ali spoke slowly, carefully, not wanting to arouse his parents' suspicions. "Faith and I wanted a chance to have some privacy in order to make certain of our decision." He smiled to take any sting out of his announcement, holding on to Faith's hand tighter to get her to stop struggling to get free.

"This is, as you know, Mother, a very important decision in my life, one I do not take lightly, and we wanted to just keep it to ourselves for a brief time, to give ourselves some time to get to know each other, to—"

"I understand, Ali." His mother glanced at her husband, her eyes filled with love. "Even though our marriage was arranged by our families, when your father and I became engaged, we went off together to simply have some time to get to know each other. It was a most wonderful time."

"Yes, son." His father's smile flashed. "This is a wise and smart thing for a young couple to do. Marriage is a very serious matter and must be undertaken with great care and consideration."

"I am so glad you understand, Father," Ali said.

"But of course, son." Omar grinned broadly at him, then at his wife. "We understand perfectly."

Omar turned to Faith, his eyes soft, his smile welcoming as he touched his hand to her cheek in such a loving, unexpected gesture, he stunned her.

"Dear one, my wife and I are honored to know that you will be joining our family and look forward to getting to know you better. We will welcome you into our home and into our hearts as our daughter and hope that one day you will love us as our son does."

"Oh." Faith's free hand went to her mouth. "What a lovely, lovely thing to say." Tears burned her eyes and she had to swallow around the lump in her throat.

They simply, automatically, accepted her, welcomed her, included her as one of them. It was unbelievable, and touched her fragile heart. In her whole life she'd never felt like she belonged anywhere, but in the space of just a few moments, Ali's parents had made her feel welcome, made her feel as if she *belonged*. Here, with them. As part of their family.

And she realized it was a wonderful, incredible feeling.

There was unadulterated joy radiating from both of them, joy that their son had finally found a mate, so how on earth could she hurt them?

How could she tell them that their only son, their pride and joy, was a lying, conniving snake in the grass, without a shred of decency or honor? A man who thought nothing of lying to the parents who adored him?

She couldn't, she realized sadly. She simply couldn't break his parents' hearts.

No matter how angry she was at Ali, or how she felt about his ridiculous lies or actions, his parents did not deserve to be hurt. And she would *not* be the one to hurt them.

However, hurting their son just might be a possibility. She tried again to tug her hand free from Ali, then realized it was probably a good thing he held her hand still or she'd probably strangle him. That'd no doubt change his parents' feelings for her!

"Faith dear." Tibi's eyes gleamed with humor. "I am thrilled with the bride my son has chosen to bring into our family." Tibi laughed. "But I must warn you, you are a brave woman to take on my son."

"Brave?" Faith cast a scathing look at Ali. "I'm not sure that's the right word for me at the moment."

Idiot was the word that came to mind. How on earth did she ever let him put her in this situation?

"Like his father, he can at times be…a handful." Tibi leaned over and gave her husband an affectionate peck on the cheek. "But you will find, my dear, that in the end it will be worth it." Tibi tenderly wiped her lipstick off her husband's cheek. "You will find the men of our family to be very loyal, very loving and very, very stubborn."

"Well, I guess one out of three isn't bad," Faith said glumly, giving Ali another scathing look and making his parents laugh.

"Ah, see, Omar dear, she is learning already."

As the waiter hesitated, dinner plates in hand, then approached, Omar stood up. "Ah, your dinner has arrived. We shall let you eat in peace."

"No, please," Ali said a bit desperately, not certain he wanted to be alone with Faith right now. He was no fool; he knew when he was in trouble. "Why don't you stay. Please? Have a drink with us?"

"I need to freshen up," his mother said, patting her hair as she, too, stood up. "Eat your dinner, children, and then we'll join you in the lounge for a nightcap later." Tibi smiled at Faith. "I am anxious to get to know you better, dear. We have much to discuss. Wedding plans to make."

"Now, Mother—"

"Hush, Ali, this is between Faith and me." She patted her son's cheek. "I have waited a very long time to plan the wedding of my only son and I am very much looking forward to it." She glanced at her husband. "Shall we go up to our room and freshen up?"

"Fine. Fine." He looked at Ali. "Son, we are most proud of you on this day." He glanced at Faith in approval. "Most proud. You have honored me and your mother with your choice of a bride, and we could not be happier."

Feeling a bit guilty, Ali stood up and shook his father's hand. "We shall see you in an hour, then?"

"Yes." Slipping his arm around his wife's waist, Omar glanced back at Faith. "Enjoy your dinner, our daughter. We will join you a bit later."

Ali watched his parents weave their way through the crowded restaurant, wishing he was going with them.

He glanced at Faith, saw the stubborn set of her jaw, the fire dancing in those glorious green eyes, the way her arms were crossed over her delicate breasts.

Ali sighed, feeling a tremor of trepidation. He had survived many, many things in his life, dangerous things, and feared nothing.

Except the anger of a woman.

He sighed again. He may be a sheik, but when it came to the heated emotions of a woman, Ali knew not even he was a match.

Seven

Prosperino, California

Shivering now as the night deepened, Emily swiped the back of her hand against her nose, then sniffled as she trudged along the shoulder of the highway, drawing her flimsy sweater tighter around her trembling body.

She was still in shock, her body drained from stark terror, her head pounding from crying.

Her knees ached from being crouched in the alcove for so many hours, and her empty stomach was rumbling, so she knew she'd been hiding in the alcove for a long time.

She had no idea how long, but she knew she had dozed off a few times, then awoken with a start, near panic when she realized what had happened.

It hadn't been a nightmare.

It was real.

Someone was trying to kill her.

She knew she couldn't stay in the alcove too much longer. The temperatures had started dropping at night, and she was dressed only in a pair of jean shorts, a T-shirt and a light sweater. The alcove was damp and cold, with a musty smell that made her nauseous.

In the echoing silence, pressed against the wall, she could hear the scurrying of night critters that burrowed under the sand. It only heightened her fear. Every sound seemed to echo loudly in her ears, making her nerves squeal ominously.

She couldn't stay in the alcove for much longer. And so she'd worked out a plan in her mind.

She'd wait until she was absolutely certain it was safe, then she'd make her way to the highway and hitch a ride—somewhere, anywhere. All she knew was that she couldn't stay here, not any longer.

She had to find someplace where she felt safe.

Only when she was certain it was clear had she slowly, carefully crept out of the alcove, checking in every direction to make sure the man hadn't waited, wasn't hiding or lurking about, waiting to grab her.

Now, forcing one foot in front of the other, she was drained and exhausted, and more than a little terrified. She had no idea what had happened tonight, no idea why anyone would try to harm her.

But she intended to find out.

Oncoming headlights had her scurrying deeper into the shoulder, stepping behind some brush so she could see, but not be seen.

Still jumpy, she had to make sure she was safe, had to make sure the person she hitched a ride with at least looked normal.

She'd never hitched before and that, too, brought its own nervousness, but she had no choice. She had exactly one dollar and forty-seven cents in her jeans. The movie tonight and pizza afterward had wiped her out.

She shook her head as she shielded her eyes from the oncoming headlights. The movie with her friends seemed like it was another lifetime ago. In reality, it was probably just a few hours.

As the vehicle drew closer, she could tell by the set of the headlights that it was a truck and a big one. This highway snaked through the entire state and was a familiar path for truckers hauling wheat to other parts of the state.

Emily sniffled, swiped at her eyes, then ran her hands over her tear-streaked face so that she looked as normal as possible.

After saying a quick, silent prayer, she stepped back out onto the shoulder, standing as close to the highway pavement as possible.

She stuck out her thumb, squinting as the headlights drew closer. The truck's horn wailed in the night, making her jump. But the driver slowed, and then finally pulled to a stop a few feet ahead of her.

Heaving a sigh of relief, Emily sprinted toward it, grateful when the passenger door opened. She glanced up into the smiling face of an elderly man.

''Well, hello there, little lady.'' He grinned, lifting his cap to scratch his white hair. ''What are you doing out here all alone at this time of night?'' He glanced around, as if looking for a disabled vehicle.

"I'm…I'm…'' Emily swallowed. "I need a ride.''

He nodded, replacing his cap. "Gathered that. Where you headed?'' He glanced at the road ahead, then glanced back at her, a soft smile on his face. "I'm heading up near Wyoming, got a haul of hay to deliver by morning.'' He watched her shiver with a worried frown.

"Wyoming?'' Emily's face brightened. Her adopted father, Joe, had grown up on a ranch in Wyoming. It seemed too good to be true.

"Yep. Then I'm heading home to the missus. Big party this weekend. The kids and the grandkiddies are all coming home. We're about to celebrate our fifty-second wedding anniversary.'' His eyes softened at the mention of his family, then he frowned as she shivered. "Lookee here, missy, it's too late and too cold for you to be out here all alone.''

"I'm going to Wyoming, too,'' Emily ad-libbed, feeling as if someone actually was looking out for her. She rubbed her hands up and down her arms.

"Are you now?'' He grinned. "Well then, why don't you ride with me a spell? You can keep me company. My name's Charley. Charley Roberts.''

"I'm Emily.''

"Just Emily?'' he asked.

"Just Emily,'' she confirmed, and he nodded again.

"Okay then, Emily, let me come around and give you a hand up. It's a mite high, specially in the dark.'' He opened his door and climbed down out of the cab, walking around the front to help her in.

"Thank you, Charley, I appreciate this.''

He chuckled softly. "It'll be nice to have the company. But I gotta warn you, I'll probably bore you to tears with stories about those grandbabies of mine." He nodded toward the dash. "You can see their pictures up there. Keep them right where I can see them all the time."

Feeling better for the first time in hours, Emily settled into the cab, sighing in relief as the warmth of the small space washed over her. She hadn't realized how cold she was until now.

She smiled when she caught the array of pictures of various children ranging in ages from babies to high-schoolers. Obviously Charley was a very proud grandfather.

The thought brought on a rush of sadness, and Emily blinked back another rash of tears. Family. It had always been so important to her, so essential, and now... Now she had no idea what was happening to her family.

To her mother.

Checking the highway for traffic, Charley paused before crossing in front of his cab, glancing at Emily through the windshield. Poor little thing. It was clear to see she was scared to death of something.

Or someone.

No doubt another runaway. Lordy, he thought with another sigh, what was the world coming to? Thank goodness he and the missus were done raising their brood. World was too scary to be raising kids nowadays.

He climbed up into the cab and settled behind the wheel, glancing in his rearview mirror before he pulled out.

"You know, Emily…" He turned to her, then smiled.

She was already fast asleep.

Prosperino, California

"What the hell do you mean she's not dead?" Meredith's voice hissed through the phone. "What the hell happened tonight? You said you were good, you said your plan was foolproof. I paid you good money, Silas, you bastard, and you blew it." Furious at this complication, Meredith blew out a breath, then dragged a hand through her still perfectly coiffed hair. "What the hell happened?" she demanded.

"She got away," Silas whined, swiping his damp palm down his jeans. "Guess she saw me before I had a chance to grab her. I was waiting in her bedroom, just like you told me, but she must have seen me, and she just took off."

"You idiot!" Nervously, she paced the length of the bedroom, glancing around carefully to make sure no one was around. She and Joe had returned awhile ago, from a day visiting with the El-Etras. Everyone was in for the night and the house was quiet. Still, that nosy housekeeper Inez was always sneaking around, listening, watching. It made her nervous. "Where the hell is she, then? She's not here."

"I don't know," Silas admitted, sniffling, then wiping his nose with the back of his hand. "She took off. I went after her, searched the grounds and stuff, but it was dark and I couldn't find her. I think she hid somewhere."

"You're an incompetent idiot," Meredith railed, pacing the floor. This was a complication she didn't need right now, not when everything else seemed about to unravel. "Listen to me carefully. You blew this and you're going to have to make this right."

"How? I don't know where she is. What do you expect me to do?"

"I don't know. Just let me think." Meredith paced, her mind spinning. "Listen," she finally said. "I think I've got a plan. She didn't come home last night, so if she saw you that means she's scared, maybe she ran. She didn't contact her father or we would have heard something by now." She walked to the bedroom door and listened. "Everyone's sleeping so obviously she didn't call here. So for right now we're the only ones who know Emily's missing. So here's what I want you to do. We're gonna pretend she's been kidnapped."

"How are you gonna do that?" he whined.

"Shut up and I'll tell you. I want you to write a note."

He scowled. "A note? What kind of note? I'm not a good writer," he complained.

"You don't have to be Hemingway to write a damn ransom note. Say you've got Emily and you're holding her for a million dollars."

"But I don't got her."

"I know that!" she snapped, rolling her eyes in frustration. "And you know that. But *they* don't know that. Joe Colton will pay any price to get one of his precious kids back. It'll seem like a drop in the bucket to him."

The thought of all that money had his attention. "So what are we gonna do with the money?"

Meredith grinned. "Split it." She wasn't giving

him a dime. It would be her own little stash, a little nest egg to help her get away if everything came tumbling down around her. Something to tide her over. Hell, she deserved it.

"All I gotta do is write a note?"

"And have it delivered here to Joe Colton." Meredith paused. "Do you think you can manage to do that without screwing it up?"

"Yeah, I think so." Silas didn't like the way she was talking to him, like he was stupid or something. "But do you think Colton will believe it?"

Meredith's eyes gleamed wickedly and she laughed. "Trust me on that. He'll believe it. I'll make sure of it."

Eight

"**Y**ou are completely and totally out of your mind," Faith raged, as she marched toward the lounge with Ali following behind. "I can't believe you lied to your parents—right to their faces! It was despicable, Ali. Absolutely despicable. Telling them we were engaged. Honestly, I could just…spit!"

She came to an abrupt halt, fists clenched, and whirled on him, causing him to nearly run into her.

"How on earth could you do that to them?" Eyes blazing, she glared at him. "They are absolutely wonderful, just wonderful, and you lied to them!"

"Faith." With a sigh, Ali placed his hands on her shoulders, shifting her out of the doorway so another couple could pass.

She flinched as if to pull away, but he held her tight. She had not stopped screeching at him from the moment his parents had left the table.

Surprisingly she hadn't run out of steam by now. She just kept going and going, like that silly little television bunny, never giving him an opportunity to explain.

He was going to take that opportunity now whether she liked it or not.

"Listen to me." He tightened his hands on her shoulders.

"There's nothing you want to say that I want to hear."

"Oh, but you are wrong, Faith dear," he said, struggling to hold on to his dwindling patience.

"Stop calling me dear." She shrugged his hands off her shoulders. In spite of her anger, his touch still made her pulse skitter wickedly, and it annoyed her to no end. Especially now.

How on earth could she have such a physical re-action to a man she found so totally reprehensible?

"I'm not your dear and I don't care what you have to say, what your reasons are. You're...you're...a jackass!"

She whirled away from him, but he caught her arm and spun her back around. Her eyes widened at the look on his face. She'd seen raging storms look calmer.

"That is enough." His voice was deep and husky, all trace of patience gone. Still holding her arm, he steered her toward a quiet corner of the bar.

"Sit," he ordered, pointing to the empty booth.

Faith felt a healthy dose of alarm. Though her own temper was simmering, she realized from his tone of voice and the dark look smoldering in his eyes that she'd gone a bit too far.

"I'll sit," she said with a haughty lift to her chin. "But not because you ordered it. I don't take orders from anyone," she clarified, sliding into the booth and shooting him a scathing glance. "Especially you."

She scooted over to the farthest side of the booth and glanced around the dimly lit room. There was a four-piece combo in the farthest corner of the lounge, playing a blues number, oblivious of the sparse sprinkling of people comprising the midweek crowd. "I'm sitting because I want to."

"Very well." Weary now, Ali slid in beside her. "I am going to try to explain this to you so that you can understand why I have done what you consider a reprehensible thing. And you are going to listen to me, Faith." He reached out and caught her chin, turning her to face him. "Do you understand me?"

"I speak English," she snapped. "Of course I understood you."

He muttered something under his breath in his native tongue. She couldn't understand it but she recognized the tremendous anger. Still she had no fear of him.

Everything she knew about him, everything she'd learned about him since they'd first met told her that in spite of his very male-oriented traditional culture, where women generally did not have the same rights or privileges as men, let alone the respect, Ali *did* have a deep and abiding respect for women, her especially. If he didn't, he would never have been able to accept her advice or business expertise. And he had, and he'd shown her nothing but deference and respect in that area, for which she was grateful.

He might infuriate her with his pompous, arrogant attitude, which she was dismayed to see had returned in full force, but he would never, ever hurt her.

Of that she was sure.

"Faith." Ali steepled his fingers and tried to put his thoughts together to explain this to her in a manner she could understand. "I love my parents very, very much."

"Then why the hell did you lie to them?" Her eyes blazed like emeralds and he could see the sheen of tears glistening on their surface. "You don't lie to someone you love."

There it was again, he realized, watching her carefully. Once before, when Faith had thought he lied to someone he cared about, someone he loved, she had worn that same look of pain, of hurt. Tears had glistened in her eyes then, too, he remembered.

Someone had lied to her, hurt her, he realized with deep sadness. Someone obviously important. But who?

Something strange and unfamiliar tugged at his gut, softened his heart. The urge to protect her, to comfort her came out of nowhere, stunning him, softening his anger at her.

"Did we not have a similar conversation once before?" he asked quietly, wanting her to understand that he was not deliberately being cruel. "Did you not jump to conclusions once before with Maureen Jourdan?"

Her anger stalled for a moment and Faith blinked away unshed tears. "But that—that was different," she stammered, wondering where he was going with this. This she hadn't misunderstood. She'd heard him lie to his parents with her own ears.

"And how can you be so sure, Faith? You are always so quick to judge me, to condemn me. Why?"

Because he looked so hurt, she felt a flash of guilt. She'd never deliberately hurt anyone.

"Do you despise me so much, Faith? Do you think so very little of me that it's easier to believe the worst than to hear the truth?" His words hung in the air for a moment.

For the first time since Jalila, he realized he did not wish to have a woman think ill of him.

Faith's opinion of him mattered, and it stunned him and alarmed him.

When had he become so concerned with her feelings, her opinions?

He could not remember.

None of the other women who had occupied his time in the past ten years had ever, ever touched his heart.

But Faith, with her viperous mouth, her independent streak, and her clear disdain for him and his entire lifestyle, had managed, somehow, to penetrate the frosty barrier of protection and wiggle her way to his impenetrable heart.

He could not—would not—allow her to matter to him, nor allow himself to be vulnerable to love, to having his heart ripped out and his life destroyed. He'd already lost a woman who had become important to him.

Never again.

"I don't despise you, Ali," Faith admitted grudgingly, honest to a fault. "I despise your actions. You lied to your parents, and I cannot and will not condone that.''

''Yes, I can understand that, Faith, but perhaps if you will listen...'' His voice trailed off. He realized he needed to phrase this correctly so that she would understand. Not because he cared about her opinion of him, he assured himself, but because she was a business associate.

''You have met my parents,'' he said carefully. ''They are...'' How did he put into words what his parents meant to him? How important they were to his life, his well-being, his very essence?

''Ali, your parents are wonderful.'' Faith touched his hand. She managed a smile, unable to bear the sudden play of emotion in his eyes.

He smiled and covered her hand with his other one, trapping hers between his, enjoying the sweet silk of her skin, the warmth of her touch.

''Yes, they are wonderful, Faith, and I love them with everything inside of me.'' He paused, glancing down at their hands. ''I would never do anything to hurt my parents,'' he said quietly, lifting his gaze to hers. ''Which is why I have lied to them.''

''You lied to them so you wouldn't hurt them?'' Faith nodded her head. ''Well, I'm sure on some planet that makes sense, but surely not this one.''

He would not be amused by her sharp tongue, he told himself, struggling with a smile. This was too important.

He took a deep breath, then continued. ''Faith, many years ago something happened in my life, something that caused me great pain.''

''Jalila.''

His head jerked up and he turned to her, struggling with the emotions Jalila's mere name had awakened.

There was such bleakness in his eyes, her heart ached for him. She recognized the bleakness only because she'd seen the same thing in her own eyes for so many years growing up.

"How did you know?" His voice was a hollow, haunting whisper.

"It's not important," she said quietly, unwilling to betray Kadid's confidence. "You loved her very much."

"Yes." He nodded slowly, wondering why he could no longer conjure up Jalila's image. For years, her face had haunted him, but now he could not seem to focus on exactly what she looked like. "We grew up together. Her father worked for mine, and our families were close. It was always expected we would marry."

"But she was killed."

He blew out a breath and glanced toward the combo in the corner, not hearing a word of the music.

"Yes." He turned to Faith and his eyes had cleared. "But since that time, my parents have worried that I will not find a suitable bride."

"So that's why they're always fixing you up?"

"Yes." He nodded again. "I am well past the age when a man in my position should have married, settled down and started a family. With each passing year, I see the fear and worry in my parents' eyes grow. The alarm that perhaps I shall end up alone. In my culture, for a man to spend his life alone, without a wife to bring him happiness, to bear him children, is a tragedy. My parents fear that I shall become the object of scorn and pity.''

"But it's only natural that your parents worry about you, Ali. They love you. They want you to be happy.''

"Yes, Faith, I understand that. Which is why I have told them this lie—about us and our engagement.'' Still covering her hand with his, he stroked a finger over her silky skin. "My parents are returning to Kuwait in just a day or two, and I thought if they believed that I had finally found a bride, then they could go back home without worrying any further about me.''

"And then of course, there is the little matter that if they thought you were engaged to someone, they'd stop fixing you up with boring blind dates.''

"Yes, there is that as well.'' Relieved, he smiled. "So you do understand.''

"I understand,'' she admitted. "That doesn't mean I like it.''

"But what harm can one little lie do if it brings contentment to my parents?''

She blew out a breath. "I don't think I can ever condone lying, but I think perhaps I understand your twisted way of thinking.''

"Last year, Faith, my father had a heart attack. It was mild,'' he rushed on at her panicked look, "but the doctors told him that he must slow down, he must learn to relax and take it easy. They ordered him to divest himself of day-to-day business interests both at home and abroad.''

"But he hasn't done it?''

"My father is a very proud and stubborn man.''

"Sort of like someone else I know."

He chuckled softly. "Yes, I suppose I am very much like my father. If he believes that I am happy, that my life is finally settled, then perhaps he will relax a bit. He needs to unburden himself of some of the responsibilities of his business, and he won't do that if he does not believe I am settled and happy. In my country, a man is not really considered an adult until he has a wife and family to care for." He lifted her hand, held it. "Do you understand now?"

"Yes," she admitted reluctantly. She didn't like the fact that after the way Ali put it, she could understand perfectly why he'd lied to his parents.

Her mind starting considering. "What happens, though, when they return to Kuwait? Your mother already wants to start planning the wedding. How are you going to get around that?"

"Quite simply, really. I will merely tell them that you have had a change of heart and decided not to marry me."

"*I* decided?" One brow rose. "So you're going to make me the bad guy in this?"

"Would you rather I said I decided not to marry you? That would rather defeat the purpose, don't you think?"

"I suppose so."

"So I am asking you, Faith, as a favor, to please do this for me. It will only be for tonight."

"You're sure?" she asked hesitantly, still not convinced she wanted to become his willing co-conspirator in this. He nodded.

"I promise." He lifted her hand, kissed it gallantly. "Just for tonight. Please?"

Faith blew out a breath, then sighed. "Ali, I don't know. I'm a computer consultant, not an actress." The thought of pretending to be his fiancée was more than a bit daunting. "I've never been a fiancée before."

He laughed, kissed her hand again. "You will do fine. I shall take care of everything."

"That's exactly what I'm afraid of," she admitted. "But okay."

"Thank you, Faith Martin. You are a wonderful woman and I am very, very grateful." He brushed his lips against hers, lightly, gently, in a teasing motion that had her eyes widening for a moment, then closing on a sigh as he deepened the kiss.

Her hands pressed to his chest, to push him away. Instead, she found her arms snaking around him, holding him close, as her lips drank deeply of his mouth.

Passion tugged, then drew them closer. Faith moaned softly as Ali slid his hand to her neck, cupping it, tilting her head to better taste her. The emotions, the feelings she had tried to deny, ignore, flared once again, reminding her how dangerous this man was to her, and her heart.

But she couldn't ignore the dangerous pull desire had on her, the feelings that erupted the moment Ali touched her, kissed her. It was a fast, heady ride that spun her around and left her dizzy.

"Here you are, children."

They jumped apart guiltily at the sound of Tibi's voice.

Still shaken, Ali looked at Faith, aroused by the earnest, innocent passion she always displayed when he touched her. One kiss, one passionate embrace, and her body was softly pliant against him, arching toward his warmth, wrapped around him in a cocoon of intimacy that made him ache for completion.

Her eyes were glazed with passion, her lips, those glorious, unpainted lips lightly swollen from his. A few strands of her hair had come loose from her ponytail, and framed her face, a face that looked as wary as a doe suddenly caught in the cross hairs.

The urge to protect, to possess came once again, as strong as the urge to mate, to make her his.

She was, he decided in that instant, a danger to him, a serious danger. He had allowed himself to let her get to him, to touch his heart, and all the places he'd vowed never to let another woman touch again.

He knew, without a doubt, he could not allow it to continue.

He wanted Faith, yes, but that was merely desire, attraction. She was a bright, intelligent woman who allowed herself to truly feel every one of life's emotions, which would make her an excellent and sensuous lover. His desire for her was perfectly natural and normal.

But there was more here, he realized, much more, and it was those other, deeper, darker emotions that frightened him.

He would have to tread carefully, to keep his own emotions under wraps.

"Mom." With a smile of welcome, Ali stood up to let his parents join them.

"Now," Tibi said with a big smile as she settled herself comfortably across from Ali and Faith. "Let's discuss the wedding."

* * *

"Would you care for another round, here?" The waitress asked, empty tray in hand as she cleared their table. The combo had quit almost an hour ago, and they were the last patrons of the evening. "It's last call," she admitted with a smile.

Ali spoke for everyone. "No, thank you. We are fine." With his arm around Faith, he felt totally comfortable and relaxed, and had to admit the evening had gone unbearably well, more so than he had ever anticipated.

He had carefully steered the conversation away from any talk of a wedding, enticing his mother instead to talk about his antics during childhood, something he knew she adored.

"It's hard to believe the evening has gone by so quickly," Tibi said, leaning her head against her husband's broad shoulder.

"Yes, I know," Faith admitted, surprised by how much she'd enjoyed herself in spite of the circumstances. "It's been wonderful." She laughed.

"You both have been wonderful to me. Thank you," she said a bit shyly, hopelessly in love with his parents already.

"Why wouldn't we be?" Omar asked, truly surprised. "Our son has presented us with a beautiful, intelligent young woman as his future bride. We are both thrilled and honored to welcome you into the family."

Faith lifted her glass to take a last sip of her cola, causing Tibi to frown.

"Faith? Where is your ring?"

Faith almost bobbled the glass. Carefully, she set

it down on the table, then glanced at Ali. "My...
ring?"

"Yes, your engagement ring." Tibi turned to Ali.
"Son, please do not tell me that you have not yet
presented Faith with a ring?" Her voice was so scan-
dalized, Ali laughed.

"No, mother, I shall not tell you such a thing." He
lifted Faith's hand, kissed it, making her squirm. He
had been totally solicitous toward her tonight, totally
warm, charming, and utterly devoted, as if they really
were engaged.

It made her realize that Ali was a great deal more
than the stubborn, arrogant man she'd come to know.
He could also be warm, charming and sweet, which
only added to her distress.

She knew that if he was not as she believed him
to be, she would have a very difficult time controlling
her feelings toward him and she could not afford to
have any feelings for him.

Too late, she thought, glancing at his handsome
profile.

"Faith's ring is at the jeweler being sized, is that
not correct, Faith?"

She swallowed. "Yes, that's correct." One little lie
had seemed to escalate into three, four, ten, until now
she couldn't seem to keep track of them. It was a
good thing they only had to do this for one night.

"So tell me, Faith, what does it look like?" Tibi
asked.

Faith opened her mouth, but no words came out.
Helplessly, she looked at Ali.

"I tried to choose something I thought would fit
Faith," he said, giving her shoulder a reassuring

squeeze as he came to the rescue. "It is a simple ring. A single diamond solitaire set in platinum. Simple, yet elegant. Like Faith." He brushed his lips across hers, making her pulse jump.

If she had been embarrassed by his kisses, his caresses in front of his parents, she had gotten over it hours ago.

She had found Ali to be naturally and openly affectionate toward her all evening, much the way she imagined a real fiancé would be.

He'd just about sent her poor system into overdrive. For the last few hours she'd begun wondering what it would be like to really be engaged to Ali, to know that he would be her husband, that she would belong to him and he to her. Forever.

The thought had sent a warm, thrilling glow through her, one she tried to contain. This was only pretend, she kept reminding herself. And just for the evening. But it was hard to remember when Ali had been so absolutely charming and attentive, making her feel wanted, appreciated, valued, *loved*. Something she never thought she'd feel with a man, for a man.

"And what about the wedding band?" his mother persisted, interested in every little detail. "What does it look like?" Her question was clearly directed at Faith.

"I don't know," she answered honestly. "I haven't seen it."

"I thought it best to save something for the wedding." Ali glanced at Faith, his gaze full of warmth and affection that made her heart turn over. "I wanted something special for that day.'' He kissed her hand. "Something as special as the day itself.''

"You've done well, my son,'' Omar said, stifling a yawn. "And we are proud, but I'm afraid I am tired. I think we shall have to say good-night.''

"Yes, it's late,'' Tibi agreed. She took Faith's hands again. "I am sorry we won't have much of a chance to get to know you better, but I have so enjoyed our time together.''

"Thank you,'' Faith said in return. "I feel the same way about you.''

Tibi smiled. "We will have plenty of time when you come home for the wedding. I shall start making plans immediately.''

Faith's heart began to pound in alarm, and she glanced at Ali, who seemed totally unperturbed by his mother's comment.

"I promise to bring Faith home in plenty of time for you to plan the wedding together.''

"Good.'' Tibi gently touched Faith's hair in a maternal fashion. "I cannot wait for some red-haired grandbabies!''

They all stood up as the lights dimmed in the lounge.

Ali gave each of his parents a hug, then draped his arm around Faith's waist, pulling her close. Unconsciously, she snuggled against him, slipping her arm around his waist, realizing how perfectly they fit together, how natural it felt to be close to him, to hold him. "I will call you in the morning.''

"Yes, please do, son,'' Omar said, taking his wife's hand. "I have a few business matters I need to discuss with you before I depart for home.''

"Until morning then," Ali said, hanging back, his arm around Faith as he watched his parents walk away.

"It went very well, don't you think?" Ali reached in his pockets for some bills, then dropped them to the table before taking Faith's arm and leading her out of the lounge.

"Well?" Faith shook her head as he guided her through the now near-empty hotel lobby toward the door that would lead them to the parking lot. She glanced at him. "I hardly consider lying and deceiving your parents as 'going well.' Your mother's already planning the wedding, and our children!" She shook her head, trying not to get swept up in all of this. "Ali, don't let this pretense linger too long."

"I know." He pushed open the door, tightening his arm around Faith as a rush of chilly night air greeted them. "But for now, they are happy." Ali paused as she pointed toward her car. "And it will stop their infernal matchmaking at least for a while."

They crossed the parking lot toward her car, his hand still on her arm.

"Faith, thank you very much for what you have done, for me, for my parents." He looked at her in the darkness, her face silhouetted by the moon, and by the smoky vapor night-lights overhead. Desire clawed at him, and he wanted to take her in his arms again.

"You're welcome." She turned to face him fully, feeling surprisingly comfortable with him. Tonight she saw none of the arrogance that so put her off. Tonight, she saw only a warm, charming man, the kind of man she'd always hoped one day to find. Quickly, she pushed the thought away.

"I know this was uncomfortable for you, but you were wonderful." Slowly, he drew her closer, holding her gaze, mesmerizing her. "You actually made them believe that we were in love," he said with a nervous laugh, making her eyes narrow.

"Something funny about that?" Faith asked with a lift of her brow, wishing she hadn't felt such a flash of hurt at his words, as if being in love with her was preposterous.

Ali lifted a hand to push a strand of windblown hair off her cheek. "Not funny, no, but ludicrous perhaps."

"Ludicrous," she repeated slowly. "And exactly what's ludicrous about it?" It hurt, she realized, deeply, and on a level she didn't think she could be hurt anymore. "Oh, I know I'm not your usual type." She said the last word with disdain.

"Type?" he repeated with a frown, realizing she was clearly upset about something. Again. "What is this type? What are you talking about? Women are women."

Her fists balled at her sides. "Typical arrogant male response. We're all the same, right?"

"No," he said carefully, realizing he was only making it worse. "You are certainly not like any other woman I know."

"And don't you think I know that? Don't you think I know I'm not someone you would generally look twice at? Let alone be someone you could fall in love with."

His gaze sharpened. "No, Faith, once again you are jumping to conclusions. It is not how I think."

"No? Then are you saying I *am* the kind of woman you could fall in love with?" Her words hung heavy in the quiet night air, reverberating softly around them. "Is that what you're saying, Ali?" She held her breath, her heart hammering, not wanting to hope, but hoping all the same.

Emotions warred within him as he looked at her, the seconds quietly ticking by as he realized he'd stepped on ground that was no more stable than shifting sand.

Loving and suffering a loss terrified him. Not even he, with all his inner strength and composure, could withstand such devastation again.

He knew it and accepted it.

Thus he knew he could never love again.

"No, Faith," he said softly, a strange ache in his heart. "You are right. I could not fall in love with you."

Nine

Wyoming

"**E**mily?" Charley Roberts gently touched her shoulder. "Emily, it's time to wake up."

She stirred, rubbed her eyes with her fists, then sat up, glancing around.

"W-where are we?" She straightened her sweater, stifled a yawn, then rubbed her cramped neck.

"Just inside the Wyoming state line. Truck stop," he said, nodding toward the low-slung one-story building with the flashing neon sign up ahead. "This is as far as I go. My delivery is just a few miles from here."

"Wyoming." Emily blinked, glancing out the window at the sky-blue horizon that seemed to go on forever.

It was all coming back now and Emily shook her head, trying to clear the cobwebs from sleep. For a moment, she thought she'd been dreaming, that the whole thing was a nightmare. But now, looking up into the Wyoming sky, and then, into Charley's kindly, homely face, she realized it wasn't a nightmare. This was reality.

Someone had tried to kill her.

And she'd run.

A shiver raced over her as she glanced out the windshield toward the diner and the parking lot filled with trucks.

At least now she was safe. No one had any idea where she was.

"Listen, it's been a long night, and I'm a mite hungry, so why don't you join me for breakfast and keep me company?" Charley frowned. She had nothing but the clothes on her back, and if he had to guess, he'd bet she didn't have but a buck or two on her.

But then most runaways never did. He couldn't very well just leave her here, at least not without filling her belly. It was the least he could do.

"Breakfast?" The thought of food made Emily's empty stomach rumble, but she thought of the piddly amount of money in her shorts pocket. Hungry or not, she wasn't certain she could afford anything, let alone to spend the last dollar she had.

"I—I don't know. I think I'd better just get going." She glanced around. There were plenty of trucks here. Surely she could hitch another ride that might get her closer to Nettle Creek.

That, she'd decided, would be her destination. Somehow it seemed a safe place to go, the place where her adopted father, Joe, had grown up. He'd loved it there, she remembered, if the stories he'd told were any indication. And it seemed a perfect place to hide out—just in case.

"Now come on, Em, you've got to eat." Charley grinned as she tied her tennis shoes. "My treat for keeping me company all night."

She laughed. "Charley, I wasn't much company. I slept most of the night."

"Maybe so, but it was company to me just the same." He laid a gentle hand on her shoulder, his eyes concerned. "Come on now, Em, I know you're running from something. I been driving this truck for too many years, seen too many runaways in my day not to recognize one. I know whatever it is you're running from, you probably think it's the end of the world, but it's not. Kids and their parents fight all the time. Heck, me and my oldest boy, Charley Jr., why we used to go at it tooth and nail all the time, but as mad as I got at that boy, I tell you, if he'd ever run off, I'd have been sick with worry." He paused, wondering how far to push. "Does anyone know where you're at?"

She shook her head. "No," she said softly.

"Well, being a father and a grandfather I can guarantee you that someone somewhere is worried senseless about you right about now." The thought had him lovingly glancing at the pictorial array on his dash, grateful his brood was home, grown and safe. "Now, no matter what your problems with your folks or your family, you should give 'em a call, just to let them know you're safe." He pulled down his visor to gather his wallet and his cigarettes, then shoved them in his shirt pocket. "Will you at least think about it?"

She nodded. But she wasn't about to call home; she didn't have a home anymore.

"Now come on, Em, I'm buying breakfast, no arguments." He grinned. "Okay?"

Emily smiled. "Okay."

"Good. Diner doesn't look like much, but they've got the best food in the state." And while they were eating, he was going to try to convince her to either go back home, or at the least, call someone to let her know where she was.

Charley threw open his door and hopped down to the pavement. "Now wait there, Emily, and I'll come down and help you."

With a quick glance around, Emily stepped into the phone booth tucked in the corner of the truck stop parking lot. Charley was right, she realized. She had to let someone know what had happened last night, where she was, and there was only one person she trusted enough to tell.

Saying a quick, silent prayer that her cousin was home, and alone, Emily dropped coins into the phone, then punched in the number by heart.

Her eyes closed and she leaned tiredly against the closed door, listening to the phone ring.

"Hello."

Emily jerked upright, unexpected tears filling her eyes at the familiar voice. "Liza, it's me, Em."

"Oh, God, Emily." Weak-kneed, Liza Colton sank down on the couch in her living room. "Where are you? Are you all right?" She pressed a hand to her throbbing forehead. "I've been worried sick about you." She had to choke back a sob.

"Liza, I'm fine, really. At least I am now." Emily's hand started to tremble, and she sank wearily against the closed door again. "Last night, Liza... Oh God, it was a nightmare, Liza. I—I'm terrified."

"Em, what the hell happened? The entire family is in an uproar. They think you've been kidnapped." Liza cleared her throat; it had grown increasingly hoarse over the past few hours.

"Kidnapped?" Shocked, Emily jerked upright. "Why on earth would they think I've been kidnapped?" She shook her head. None of this made sense.

Liza gripped the receiver tighter, tucking her long legs under her. "Your father called to say a ransom note was delivered to him this morning. Everyone in the family is just beside themselves."

"What? My God, I don't believe it." She shook her head. "Why would anyone deliver a ransom note to my dad when I haven't been kidnapped?"

"Are you sure you're all right?" Liza asked again, not certain what was going on, but wanting to be certain that her cousin was truly safe.

"Yes. But something did happen last night. Something awful."

"I knew it." Tears spilled from Liza's eyes and her hands started to tremble. "I knew something was terribly wrong. You were supposed to call me last night, and when I didn't hear from you..." Her voice trailed off.

"Liza, this is all bizarre. I don't know what the heck's going on." Emily glanced up at a heavyset man heading toward the phone booth. She'd have to make this quick. "Liza, listen to me. I don't have long to talk. I'm at a pay phone in Wyoming—"

"Wyoming? Emily, what are you doing in Wyoming?"

"Last night when I got home no one was home. The house was dark. I let myself in, then went upstairs. My bedroom door was partially closed."

"Why?" Liza frowned. "Your bedroom doors are never closed unless everyone's in for the night."

"Exactly. I pushed open the door just a bit to see in but not be seen." Emily took a deep breath, pressed a hand to her heart as if she could slow its suddenly raging beat. "Liza, there was a man in my bedroom, with a knife, waiting for me."

"Oh God, Emily. Oh God." Letting her head fall to her hand, Liza tried to stop the well of tears. "What did you do?"

"I ran, Liza. And hid in the alcove. You remember the alcove we used to play in as kids?"

"Sure."

"I hid in there for hours, until it was safe and I was sure the guy was gone." Rubbing her brow, Em nervously glanced around the parking lot. The heavyset trucker had stepped into the phone booth next to her. "When I was sure it was safe, I crept out and headed toward the highway. I hitched a ride and I'm in Wyoming. I had to leave, Liza. I didn't think it was safe to stay at home any longer."

"Emily, what is going on?" Liza swiped at her eyes and shook her head. "None of this makes any sense."

"I know. Why would someone send a ransom note to my dad when I haven't been kidnapped?"

Absently, Liza rubbed her sore throat again. "I don't know, Em."

Emily's mind whirled as she tried to put the pieces together. "It had to be someone who knew I didn't come home last night. Someone who felt I wouldn't be home for a while. Otherwise, they'd never have been able to feel comfortable sending that ransom note. I mean, it would be pretty hard to claim I've been kidnapped if I came sauntering in the house this morning." She twisted the phone cord, thinking.

"You think the ransom note and the guy who tried to kill you are connected?"

"Has to be," Emily concluded. "There's no other explanation. No one knows where I'm at, or that I've left California—except the guy who was chasing me. He knows I disappeared, so he told whoever he was working for, and they thought they'd make a quick buck off of it."

"What are you thinking, Emily?" Liza's eyes widened. "You don't think…your mother…"

Emily frowned. "Liza, listen to me, someone tried to kill me last night and I don't know why. Someone's sent a ransom note to my father, and I don't know why. Nothing has been the same in my life since the day of the accident. Meredith changed that day into someone neither of us knows. Other than you, who else knew I was going to a movie with friends last night? Who else knew that I'd be coming home to an empty house?"

"Oh God, Em, what are we going to do?"

"For now, I'm going to stay in Wyoming and out

of sight. I want a chance to see if I can get to the bottom of this.''

''Okay.''

''Now Liza, listen to me. You and I are the only ones who suspect there's something seriously wrong with Meredith.''

''Yeah, so?''

''So.'' Emily blew out a breath and chose her words carefully. ''So if any of this has anything to do with the fact that we suspect there's something wrong with Meredith, that means you might be in danger as well. Please, please be careful.''

A chill washed over Liza. ''I will. I promise.''

''Don't tell anyone where I am. For now, let them think I've been kidnapped. I'll get in touch with you when I can. I'm headed to Nettle Creek so I'll—'' Emily frowned. ''Liza, aren't you leaving on tour tomorrow?''

Liza sighed. She dreaded the grueling singing tour she was to face, thanks to her strict manager, her mother Cynthia. ''Yes, but you know my schedule.'' She inhaled deeply, rubbing her throat again. ''Oh, Emily, I'm so scared for you.''

''Don't be.'' Emily forced the worry from her voice. ''I'm fine, really. I figure I'll get a job in Nettle Creek, and an apartment, and see if I can do some digging from there. Please don't worry, Liza, I'll be fine.''

''I hope so.'' Liza tried to think. ''Do you want me to wire you some money?''

''Wait until I get an address you can send it to.''

Liza sighed. ''Okay. But please be careful and take care of yourself.''

"I will. As soon as I can I'll let you know where I am."

"Okay, please. And, Em?"

"Yeah?"

"I love you."

Emily smiled. "I love you, too, Liza. You be careful and take care of yourself, too. Good luck on the tour."

"Yeah, thanks." There wasn't much enthusiasm in her raspy voice. She sighed heavily. "I'm not looking forward to it and will be glad when it's behind me." She had to clear her throat again, fearing she was losing her voice. Her mother would be furious.

"Look, Liza, I gotta go. I'll be in touch." Quietly, Emily hung up the phone, then pressed her fingers to her burning eyes to stop the tears. Lifting her head, she touched the phone, said a prayer for her cousin, then stopped out of the phone booth and glanced around, looking for a ride that would take her into Nettle Creek, where hopefully, she'd be able to put the pieces of this puzzle together and find some safety.

And some answers.

Ten

Faith heard the commotion in her outer office, but didn't pay any attention to it. She was weary and exhausted from a sleepless night of crying.

After the scene with Ali last night in the parking lot, after he admitted she was not the kind of woman he could love, she'd lain awake all night, cursing herself for her sheer stupidity.

She'd allowed him to use her last night, to use her to deceive his parents, something she knew was wrong, and yet she'd let him persuade her with what seemed like logic at the time.

The man touched her, and she lost her head.

Shades of her mother, she thought with a sigh, feeling worse by the minute.

Sometime during the night she realized that she simply couldn't bear to see Ali again, to be in his presence, not knowing what she knew, not knowing what kind of man he was, and what kind of woman she became when she was with him.

Not knowing how he truly felt about her.

Or rather couldn't feel about her.

She refused to admit that somewhere along the line her feelings for Ali had changed into something she couldn't even bear to acknowledge.

So this morning, instead of going to the investment house to finish working on his system, she sent one of her best consultants. She didn't ever want to see Ali again if she didn't have to.

Instead, she'd come into the office to finish some much-needed paperwork, certain if she stayed busy, she could ease the ache in her heart.

She heard Martha's deep, booming voice and smiled to herself, confident her office manager could handle whatever problem had apparently cropped up.

Martha had been with her since the day she'd opened the office seven years ago, although Faith still wasn't certain who had hired whom.

At the time, she'd been advertising for almost a week and had had no responses. Martha had walked in, taken one look around at the chaos and announced it would do. She'd been with Faith ever since.

With the looks of Stalin, the bulldog determination of Churchill, and the cantankerousness of Patton, Martha could handle anything and anyone.

So Faith was more than surprised when her office door flew open and Martha stood there huffing like a peacock who'd just gotten its feathers plucked.

"Man's an imbecile. Determined as can be. He

won't leave and he won't take no for an answer. But I'll handle him. Just don't you mind the commotion.''

"Man?" Faith glanced up with a frown. "What man?"

"That man." Martha jerked a finger over her shoulder, moving back and forth in the doorway to block his path so he couldn't sneak past her. He was standing right behind her, breathing down her neck. "Doesn't understand I can't be letting in all kinds of riffraff."

"'Riffraff'." The man's deep, booming voice was laced with outrage.

Ali.

Faith heaved a deep, heartfelt sigh, then rubbed her weary eyes. She didn't want him here.

"My good woman, do you have any idea to whom you are speaking?"

Faith rolled her eyes at his imperious, highfalutin tone. She was used to it by now, and simply ignored it. Martha, on the other hand, was a whole other kettle of fish.

If Ali had any brains at all, he wouldn't be using that tone of voice with Martha, who did not take kindly to anyone with an attitude or without an appointment.

"No, but I got me a feeling you're going to tell me who you are, aren't you?" Martha asked with a weary sigh, planting thick hands on her even thicker waist.

Ali's spine stiffened. "My good woman, I am Sheik Ali El-Etra, a member of the Kuwati royal family." Arrogant outrage sharpened every word, making Faith sigh once again. Anyone else would have been quaking in their shoes at that haughty tone. Not Martha.

She merely gave him a friendly pat on his shoulder. "Well, I'm sure you're rightly proud of yourself, but all that fancy stuff doesn't amount to a hill of beans here in *this* office. In this office, no one gets in to see Ms. Martin without an appointment. And you ain't got one, so you're not getting in and I don't give a fig's fart if you're the Queen Mum herself."

"My good woman—"

"Trust me, I ain't that good and I got four ex-husbands to attest to it."

Ali's temper simmered. "How dare you speak to me in such a manner. I can assure you I am not accustomed to such disrespect."

"Well then, maybe it's about time you got accustomed to it."

Frustrated, Ali closed his eyes and inhaled a slow, deep breath. He would not be beaten by this... woman. He had to see Faith.

He glanced at the woman who was almost as wide as the doorway. Intimidation hadn't worked; he certainly hoped charm would. He flashed her a brilliant smile, hoping she'd take pity on him.

"Martha, please, it is imperative that I see Ms. Martin." He was playing bob and weave with a woman the size of a Sherman tank. It was utterly outrageous, and beneath him to be reduced to such behavior. "It really is a matter of the utmost urgency. And I am a client," he reminded her.

"A client?" Martha narrowed her gaze on him. "If you were a client, I'd know about you, and I've never heard of you."

"El-Etra Investments."

She cocked her gray head, narrowing her gaze on him suspiciously. "Yeah, what about 'em?"

"I am the owner."

"You are not." She searched her memory. "Kadid something or other is the owner."

Ali bit back a smile. "On the contrary, Kadid is my assistant. He is the one who made all the arrangements to hire Ms. Martin, but I can assure you, I am indeed the owner."

Martha scowled at him. "You got a card or something on you?"

"Or something." Ali reached into his breast pocket and pulled out an elegant business card with his name, family crest and royal seal etched in gold.

"Guess anyone who can afford to have them fancy business cards printed up must be telling the truth." Martha glanced at Faith over her shoulder. "Okay, you got five minutes, and not a minute more. Ms. Martin's busy."

"As am I," he countered in annoyance. He had been up most of the night, worried about what he'd said to Faith, worried that perhaps she'd misinterpreted what he'd said, and more importantly, worried that he'd hurt her.

The look in her eyes last night, the crushing sadness when he'd admitted he could not love her had haunted him long into the night.

He'd hurt her, he realized now, and he never intended to, never meant for her to take his comments personally. But from the look on her face when she quietly got into her car and drove away, he knew she had.

Miserable, he'd vowed somehow to make it right this morning.

But when he'd arrived at the office this morning he'd found some young, pimply-faced...*child* working on his system. First he had panicked, then became enraged. He could not allow Faith to simply walk out of his life. Not like this.

"Thank you, Martha," he said with a relieved sigh as she stepped out of the doorway to let him pass. "I am grateful." With an elegant bow, he lifted her hand and kissed it.

"Quit your bowing," Martha said a scowl. "And don't be slobbering all over me. I got work to do." With an annoyed humph, she marched toward her own desk.

Faith didn't even bother to glance up when Ali walked in. She knew he was there. The air had changed; it had become charged with his potent male energy. "What do you want? I'm busy." Her tone was cold, clipped and all business.

"What do I want?" His voice shook with outrage. "I want to know why you are here in this office, instead of mine."

She continued working on the spreadsheet. "Someone is at your office. One of my best consultants. Peter is more than competent to complete the job." Now she did glance up at him for a brief moment. Her gaze was deliberately cold. "On time as we agreed. You have nothing to worry about."

"On the contrary, Faith. I have plenty to worry about, as do you."

Now her head came up and she glared at him, trying not to notice how tired he looked this morning. "What are you talking about?"

Trying to control himself, Ali planted his hands on her desk. "Listen to me very carefully, Faith. For whatever reason you decided not to return to my offices this morning. But my contract is with *you.* I agreed to hire you, personally because I was told *you* were the best. If I wanted a subordinate, I would have hired him. I have no intention of putting my business in the hands of someone who is not yet even old enough to vote."

"You're being ridiculous. Peter is twenty-six, graduated Phi Beta Kappa from Harvard, and has an MS from Yale. He's one of the best computer consultants in the country."

"But he is not you, is he?"

"It doesn't matter, you don't need me. Peter can do the job."

"No, he cannot," Ali retorted just as firmly. "It is still my office, still my decision whom I allow into it. I have some highly classified financial information on that system, information about very wealthy individuals around the world. You certainly cannot expect me to entrust that kind of information to just anyone."

"You're being ridiculous, Ali."

"Perhaps. But that's my prerogative. I *am* the client, and the one paying the bills. And I believe you have a saying in America, 'the client is always right'?"

"The customer's always right," she corrected. Faith sighed. She knew they weren't really arguing about Peter's credentials or the security of his firm, but something far more personal.

"I'm too tired to argue with you, Ali." She pressed her fingers to her tired eyes for a moment, wishing they'd stop burning. "Just tell me what you want."

You, an inner voice whispered, but he ignored it. He could not, would not voice such a preposterous statement.

She looked exhausted, he realized, feeling his anger soften. As exhausted as he felt. There were dark shadows of fatigue under her eyes, which, this morning, looked oddly swollen, as if she'd been crying.

He felt an enormous flicker of guilt, and wondered if he'd been the cause of those tears.

At the moment, he wanted only to reach for her, to enfold her in his arms, to inhale her sweet scent, to feel her womanly curves pressed against him, to let his lips brush hers, to feel her heart beat next to his.

To comfort her, he told himself. Merely to comfort her.

He straightened, slipping his hands in his pockets, fearing he'd reach for her if he didn't. Right now he wanted to apologize and explain his comments last night.

But he knew he could not. He would never be able to admit to her that he, Sheik Ali El-Etra *feared* falling in love. For a man to admit he feared something was to admit he was a coward. It was totally out of the realm of anything he'd ever learned in his life. Men did not admit fear. Ever. Especially a man in his position.

"What do I want, Faith?" He smiled slowly. "I

want what I contracted for—your services. Yours, not someone else's.''

"You can't have me.'' She feared she hadn't the defenses to deflect his charm, his appeal, and she didn't want to make a fool of herself again.

His eyes darkened. "That is the second time you have told me that I cannot have you, and I will tell you again, you are wrong, Faith. Very wrong. And on this, I suggest you don't push me, because I will push back. Hard.''

"What are you talking about?''

He glanced at his watch. "If you are not in my offices at work on my system by noon today, I will instruct my attorneys to file a breach of contract suit against you and your firm. I will also instruct them to file an immediate injunction preventing you from personally working anywhere else until you have completed the work you were contracted for at El-Etra Investments.''

Shock nearly stole her breath and she gripped the edge of her desk until her knuckles whitened.

"You can't be serious!'' Just the thought of a lawsuit made her feel faint. If word got out that she'd been sued for breach of contract by a client, especially a client of Ali's magnitude, she'd lose all credibility in the business community.

"Ali,'' she whispered, her face pale, "you can't honestly be serious about this.'' Not even he would stoop so low.

Would he?

One dark brow arched. "Do you really want to test how serious I am, Faith?'' Ali glanced at his watch again. "Noon, Faith. Be there. Or be prepared for the consequences."

It was almost five in the afternoon before Ali could get free to go down to the systems room to see Faith. He knew she'd returned to his offices, exactly five minutes before noon, because Kadid had informed him immediately.

Aware that something had happened between them, Kadid had discreetly been keeping an eye on Faith all afternoon, then reporting to Ali her progress and her mood.

From all accounts, Ali decided, she was probably about ready to kill him.

He almost smiled. She was the most cantankerous, obstinate, independent woman he'd ever met, with a stubborn streak as wide as his.

He adored her.

But she was not going to be pleased when she saw him or heard his news.

Sighing deeply, Ali stood in the doorway, listening to the hum of machines, watching her hunched over a keyboard, much the same way he had the first day he'd come down here.

He wanted to go to her, stroke a hand down her hair, rub the tension from her shoulders. He resisted, knowing he'd probably get a black eye for his efforts.

"Faith." He walked into the room, saying her name so he wouldn't startle her.

"I'm here, I'm working as we contractually agreed." Her voice was cool and impersonal. She continued with what she was doing, not even sparing him a glance. "However, there is nothing in our contract that states I have to see you or speak to you."

"You are absolutely correct," he said, coming around the desk to stand in front of her so he could see her. She looked even more weary than she had this morning. "You do not have to see me or speak to me." She didn't acknowledge him or glance at him. "But I do think you're being a bit childish and churlish."

His words caused her temper to simmer. "I tend to get a bit churlish when someone threatens me."

"And is that what I did, Faith, threaten you?"

"Strong-arm me is more like it." She had to concentrate, so she concentrated on putting her anger into the machine she was working on.

"I'm sorry you feel that way." Absently, Ali glanced at her, noted her shoulders had tensed even further. "Do you hate working here so much, Faith?" His voice was whisper-soft, sending a shiver over her, making her more annoyed with herself than ever.

She had to take a deep breath and bite her tongue so she wouldn't say something perfectly vile and vicious, even if he did deserve it.

"I hate that you've used me to deceive your parents." Now she looked up at him so he could see the anger radiating in her eyes. He saw something else as well—pain. He wasn't certain he could bear knowing that he was the one who had caused that pain.

"I hate the fact that you threatened and bullied me to get your own way. I hate the fact that you're an arrogant, impossible snob who thinks the world owes him something because of who he is." She had to take a deep breath because her voice was shaking and she didn't want him to know how close to tears she was. "And I especially hate the fact that you think women are disposable. Here solely for your use and your pleasure, to be discarded when you're through with them."

"Is that what you truly think of me, Faith?" he asked quietly, truly appalled at her opinion of him. He stood up, came closer. "Is that what you think I did to you? Used you, then discarded you?"

She wasn't going to cry. "You used me to deceive your parents."

"This is sadly true, but I thought perhaps you understood my reasoning. My intention was not cruelty, but love. I thought you understood that." When she didn't answer, he went on. "Do you really hate being here and working for me so much?"

"I don't want to be here," she said simply, unwilling to explain. Let him think what he wanted.

"What if I offered to make a deal with you? Give you an out so you would not have to come back here ever again. You could let your young man, Peter, come back if you so liked." He was taking a chance, and a big one, but at this point he had nothing to lose.

Her heart filled with a mixture of hope and dread. Hope that this misery would end, that she didn't have to see him every day and be reminded that she was not the kind of woman he could love.

Dread that if she wasn't here she might not ever see him again. And she didn't know if she could bear it.

But wasn't that what she wanted?

"I don't make deals with the devil."

He laughed. "You signed a contract with one, if

I'm the devil you are referring to. I think it is a bit late to get moralistic now."

She considered for a moment, too tempted not to find out what he was proposing. "What kind of deal are you talking about?" she asked suspiciously.

He was quiet for a moment. "I just spoke to my mother. They were so impressed with you, they've decided to extend their visit for a few days. They've invited us to spend the weekend with them at their home in Palm Springs. We would leave late tomorrow afternoon."

"Are you crazy?" She shot to her feet. "How dare you even suggest such a thing." Totally enraged, she was shaking. "It's out of the question. I'm not play-acting or pretending to be your doting, obedient wife-to-be, nor am I going along with a continued deception of your parents. It's out of the question."

"Faith." He took a step closer, and she was grateful the desk separated them. "Please hear me out. This is obviously important to me. You know how I feel about my parents. And I am very, very grateful to you for the part you played in easing their mind and bringing them some happiness."

"You're not going to soften me by playing on my sympathies," she stated, crossing her arms across her chest.

But Ali could see she was weakening, and a pinch of hope flared.

"I understand that perhaps I have done things... said things that maybe you have not understood or approved of, things that, at times, seemed less than honorable, but I hope you will know and believe, that I am a man of honor, of integrity, and I would never knowingly hurt someone, especially my parents.''

''I don't know any such thing.'' Her voice was not as strong as she would have liked. In spite of her anger, her hurt, she couldn't deny what he said was the truth. His intentions were honorable, his methods were just screwed up.

What hurt was the truth, the truth that she was good enough to play-act the part of his wife-to-be, but she was not a woman he could ever love.

For an instant Faith wondered if her anger was really a bruised ego.

''My parents are deeply fond of you, Faith, and with good reason. You are an incredible woman, and I admire you a great deal.'' The suspicion in her eyes increased, making him sigh.

Wonderful. He admired her. It made her spirits sink further. That was the equivalent of going on a blind date in college and being told your date had a ''great personality.'' It was the kiss of death.

''Faith, if you will agree to do this for me, you will earn my eternal gratitude.''

''With that and a dollar I can maybe buy a cup of coffee.'' She didn't want his gratitude, what she wanted, she realized, was something he'd already admitted he couldn't give her. His love.

Why was it so important, she wondered, finally looking at him. It struck her then, like a spirited arrow to the heart.

She was, God help her, in love with him.

The knowledge staggered her simply because she had no idea when it had happened, had no idea when she'd let herself care so deeply.

How much of a fool could she be? Loving a man who'd already admitted he could never love her.

Perhaps she hadn't learned as much from her mother's mistakes as she thought. Or perhaps, she thought with an inward sigh, she was destined to make the same mistakes.

"Faith?" He waited until the troubled look in her eyes cleared before continuing. "If you go with me to my parents' this weekend, I will release you from your contract and allow your colleague to finish the job. I will also make sure that Abner Josslyn knows what a fine job you have done for El-Etra."

Her mind and her heart were still reeling. Once the job was over, Ali would be out of her life for good. This weekend might be the last chance she had to be with him, to see him. It might be all she'd ever have.

But she wasn't about to make it easy for him. "I still get the bonus if Peter finishes the job?"

"But of course." He smiled, more relieved than he believed possible.

"I also want a glowing letter of recommendation personally signed by you."

"Done."

"And I want tomorrow morning off."

"What?" Her request took him by surprise. "I do not understand."

"I need to go shopping, Ali. I have no intention of going to your parents' home for the first time without bringing a proper gift for the hostess. And I'll need time to shop."

Pleased beyond measure that she was going away with him, he smiled at her. "It is a lovely gesture, Faith, truly, but not necessary."

One brow rose. "I don't believe I asked for your opinion."

He chuckled, wondering if he'd ever get accustomed to her sharp tongue. He hoped not, it was charming. "No, this is true, you did not."

"When I do want your opinion, I'll ask for it. Until then, please keep it to yourself. Now if you're through, I've got work to do." She sat down.

"As do I." Overjoyed, he laid his hand over hers, causing her pulse to speed up. "Thank you, Faith. You have no idea how much this means to me." He stroked her hand, aching to touch her softness. He had a reprieve, a whole weekend to try to make things right with her. "I shall phone my parents and tell them we'll be there in time for dinner."

"You do that," she said.

"And, Faith, I would just like to say that it would be wise to remember that we are supposed to be engaged. It would not look good if we were hissing and spitting at each other all weekend. In spite of everything, we should at least try to be…friends. And perhaps we will enjoy each other's company this weekend."

"Don't bet the farm on that one."

"What farm?" he asked with a frown, making her laugh.

"Never mind. It's just an expression."

"Do you agree, Faith, that we might at least try to be friends?"

"Well, I normally don't befriend people who threaten and blackmail me, but I have made a deal, so I'll honor it." She sighed in resignation. "I'll be sweet, civil and obedient."

"Ah, the perfect woman," he said, making her glance up at him sharply. Holding up his hands, he laughed at the storm clouds of indignation gathering in her beautiful eyes. "I was only kidding, Faith. With you, somehow, I don't think the words sweet and obedient would be used in the same sentence. At least not by me."

"Dogs are obedient. Cookies are sweet. Women are human." She raised her chin a notch. "You'll do well to remember that."

He felt once again the heat that always seemed to leap between them, drawing them closer, entangling them. How on earth was he going to get through an entire weekend with her without making a fool of himself?

He honestly didn't know.

"I'll pick you up tomorrow afternoon."

His hands itched to touch her, so he slipped them back in his pockets. He had to leave, fearing if he didn't, he'd do something they might both regret.

Eleven

"**W**hat? What? What is this mess?" Pierre, hair stylist extraordinaire plucked up bunches of Faith's long hair and frowned in disdain as he ran his fingers the length of the dry strands. "Did you use a lawn mower to cut this?" Another clump. "Or perhaps a weed whacker? No, no, I've got it, pruning shears, correct?" One brow rose imperiously and he scowled down his perfectly sculptured nose at Faith, who was doing a little scowling of her own.

"Can you fix it?" she asked, wondering for the tenth time what she was doing here. She knew what she was doing, but still, it annoyed her. As long as she was going to spend the weekend with Ali's parents, and since she was supposed to be his fiancée, she figured she might as well play the part and at least try to look like the kind of woman he should be engaged to.

She couldn't very well show up at his folks in Palm Springs in torn jeans and a T-shirt, let alone her hair in a ponytail. She'd have looked like a ragamuffin, as Martha told her when she'd insisted Faith come to see Pierre.

It was Martha who had made the appointment at this very chic, very expensive day salon where she would be made over from head to toe. Insisted, nagged and forced was more like it, Faith thought with a scowl, pushing back a strand of hair from her face.

Martha had booked her for a full day's treatment— whatever that meant. All she knew was that she was going to have people tugging, pulling and fussing over her all day and she just hoped she had the patience for all this nonsense.

It wasn't that she didn't enjoy looking good or feminine, she just felt it was a horrific waste of time and money to do all the boringly feminine things required to look like she stepped out of a fashion magazine.

She had so many more important things to do with her time and money. Faith blew out a breath and garnered some patience. She'd promised Martha, she reminded herself, and if the truth be known, she was actually looking forward—just a little bit—to seeing what kind of magic, if any, Pierre and his troops could do.

She knew she was scheduled to have her hair cut and styled, colored perhaps as well. A makeup artist was going to paint her face, but teach her how to do it as well. A manicure and a pedicure, as well as something called a mud wrap. Why she was paying good money to have someone wrap her in mud was a mystery.

She glanced at Pierre through the mirror in front of her. He was still scowling over her hair. "Can you fix it?"

"Fix it?" He fairly shuddered. "My dear, that's my job." His chin lifted as he continued to glare at her head. "By the time I'm finished with you, even your mother wouldn't recognize you." He bent and lifted one of her hands. "Mercy, you obviously have found more than one use for those pruning sheers."

"I work with my hands," she said, snatching her hand back and tucking it under her leg so he couldn't see it.

"A ditch digger, perhaps?" he asked, then smiled, retrieving her hand. "Please don't worry my dear." He patted her hand affectionately. "I can see that you haven't had the time or the inclination to do the things necessary to make yourself beautiful."

"Beautiful?" She gaped at him. He was either blind, or a very bad liar. No one had ever called her beautiful before.

His smile widened and his eyes softened. "Yes, dear, beautiful." He tipped her chin up. "Very," he added softly as his gaze studied every inch of her delicate features. "You've just never had anyone to teach you how to make the most of your beauty." He clapped his hands together. "But I'll teach you, dear, and before the day is out, you'll not recognize yourself."

Faith scooted lower in the chair, staring at her familiar reflection. *Not recognize herself?* She scooted lower. That's exactly what she was afraid of.

* * *

She hadn't actually meant to buy new clothes, it was an impulse really. She'd been out shopping for a proper present to bring Ali's parents, and was merely window shopping, looking at all the lovely fall clothes on display in the store windows.

She hated skirts and dresses, hated all that female fussiness, but she'd spotted a beautiful silk pantsuit in a shade of green that caught her eye.

On impulse, she'd gone in and tried it on. It fit like a glove. Smelling a sale, the saleswoman had brought in several other pantsuits in sparkling fall colors, insisting Faith try on each and every one.

In the end, she'd walked out of there with three new outfits, and since she had no other shoes but her tennis shoes, she headed to a shoe store.

As luck would have it, they not only were having an enormous sale, but she found shoes in almost the same shade as her new outfits.

Pleased, and now running late, she'd dashed home to shower, change and pack her new things.

A littler nervous about her appearance, when she spotted Ali's car in the driveway, she pulled open the door.

He was halfway up the drive before he realized she was standing in the doorway. His brain fogged and he blinked. Once. Twice.

"Faith?" Her hair was down, spilling to her shoulders in a wild tangle of fiery curls. The outfit she had on was a beautiful jade-green that matched her eyes and hugged her figure in a way that had his breath backing up in his lungs.

"It's me," she said, pleased by his response. She could have kissed Martha in gratitude.

He took her hands in his, noticing they were trembling. She's nervous, he thought with an inward smile, totally disarmed by her. "You look absolutely beautiful."

Beautiful. Closing her eyes for a moment, she savored the word. No one had ever told her she was beautiful before, and at this moment, with the way he was looking at her she felt beautiful.

She would never want to compete with all the beautiful women he dated and romanced; she was not in the least bit interested in becoming a revolving mannequin for some designer in order to impress a man. She had far more important things to do with her time and money.

But that didn't mean she couldn't dress up when the situation required it. Especially if this was the response she got.

"Thank you," she stammered a bit self-consciously, running a damp hand down her thigh.

"Let me get your bags." He couldn't take his eyes off her. The outfit was neither daring nor revealing, but classic and elegant in spite of its tailored design.

It was absolutely perfect for her, on her. It wasn't just that her beautiful hair was down, either. It was something more.

Perhaps it was just seeing her like this, outside of the work environment, outside of her usual jeans. Why had he not realized that she was beautiful in her own distinct way?

He grabbed her bags while she locked up, then took her arm as he guided her toward his car.

Scowling, she came to a halt right at the edge of the driveway. "Ali, what is this thing?"

He shook his head, following her gaze. "I do not understand. What do you mean?"

She nodded toward his car. "What is that?"

"This is a car, Faith," he said with some confusion, opening the back and depositing her luggage.

"No," she said, pointing to her sensible four-door compact parked in the street. "That's a car." She turned back to him, pointing at the screaming fire-engine red contraption in her driveway. "This is a can opener with a removable cover."

He laughed. "Faith, you are the only woman I know who would call a two-hundred-and-fifty-thousand-dollar Maserati a can opener with a removable cover."

She almost dropped her small clutch purse. "You paid a quarter of a million *dollars* for a car that doesn't even have a back seat?" Shock had her voice edging upward. "For that kind of dough they could have at least thrown in a back seat, two and a half baths, and a two-car garage."

"Faith, it is a two-seater roadster. Imported and custom-made. It's not supposed to have a back seat."

Most women adored this exquisite, expensive vehicle. She merely wrinkled her nose in disdain. Would she never stop surprising him?

When they were in the car, Ali said, "Now, Faith, you cannot start out this weekend scowling." Smiling, he traced a finger down her nose. "It will spoil the trip. I thought we'd drive along the coast, take our time and enjoy the wonderful afternoon. It will give us a chance to talk."

"Talk?" Faith repeated as if she'd never heard the word before.

"Yes, you know, exchange pleasantries, pretend we are having a good time." He reached out and covered her hand. She looked at his hand, so strong, so masculine, and yet so gentle over hers. "After all, we are supposed to be engaged, remember?"

How on earth could she forget? She wouldn't be here now, with him, if she wasn't pretending to be something she wasn't, something she could never be.

Blowing out a breath, she ordered herself to relax. She had agreed to this charade and she might as well make the best of it.

"I bought you a present," he said a bit mysteriously.

"A present?" she repeated with a wary scowl.

He laughed. "Faith, you are the only woman I know who would be suspicious of a gift. Most women would be thrilled."

"Well, in case you haven't noticed, Ali, I'm not most women."

"I've noticed," he said quietly, letting his gaze scan her features, sending a shiver racing over her with his dark, intense look.

With a smile, he reached to the floor, lifted a brown paper bag and handed it to her.

"Open it."

"Nothing's going to jump out at me, is it?"

Shaking his head, he laughed. "Faith, you are precious." He flipped on his directional, expertly changing lanes, then glanced at her. "Trust me, nothing will jump out at you." He waited a beat, until she'd unfolded the top of the bag. "Probably," he added with an amused smile, watching her back away from the bag warily, making him laugh once again.

"Open it, I promise you will like it."

"Why are you buying me presents?" she asked, stalling.

He shrugged. "Why not? A man should buy presents for his betrothed."

"Ali, this is pretend, remember? We're not really engaged, and presents aren't necessary."

"Ahh, but trust me, this present is." He nodded toward the bag. "Open it."

With another suspicious glance in his direction, Faith opened the bag, then laughed. "Oh, Ali."

Touched, she pulled out two cold cans of cola, a bag of chips and two candy bars, holding them up like a trophy.

"The sustenance of life," he said, delighted by her response.

"You remembered?"

"I remember every single thing you've ever told me." He glanced in his rearview mirror as he overtook a pickup truck, then turned back to her, his gaze soft, serious. "And everything you have not yet told me."

She popped the top on one of the cola cans, handing it to him. "What do you mean?"

Carefully, he sipped his drink, then slid it into the cup holder. "You told my mother that you spent some time at the Hopechest Ranch."

Faith sipped her own drink, wondering where he was going with this. "Yes, that's true. I did."

"Why?" With a frown, he glanced at her. "Where were your parents? Your family?"

He watched her face change, her body stiffen.

"I don't have a family." The flatness of her tone had him cocking his head, looking at her curiously.

The change in her expression caused him to study her more carefully. There was pain there, he realized, pain and something else shadowing those gorgeous green eyes.

He closed his hand over hers now, engulfing it in his, warming her with his touch. "Everyone has a family, Faith," he said gently, not wanting to pry, but wanting to know what had caused such pain.

He'd seen it before, both times when she'd thought he'd deliberately lied to someone he loved.

Obviously something very troubling had happened to her, something very troubling indeed.

It touched his heart, made him sad and curious to see her looking so fragile, so vulnerable. His protective instincts were so strong, especially when it came to Faith, he had to curb the urge to swing the car over to the shoulder and take her in his arms and just hold her.

"No," she corrected, her voice slightly brittle. "Not everyone has a family. I don't."

She didn't like talking about her past, especially her family, if that was what you wanted to call it.

She'd worked hard, very hard to overcome all the anguish of her childhood and she certainly didn't want to start dredging it up and all the painful memories with it.

"Tell me about it," he said quietly, stroking her hand in a soothing gesture, encouraging her to talk to him. "Do you have brothers and sisters?" he asked when it was clear she was not going to volunteer the information.

She shook her head.

"So you are an only child, like me."

She almost choked. "Like you?" Laughing, she shook her head, but there was no humor in her laughter. How on earth could he even imagine they had *anything* in common? "Hardly."

"But you are an only child?"

"Yes."

"But so am I."

"But I guarantee you that's where the similarities end."

"What about your mother? Surely you have a mother?"

Realizing he wasn't going to let it drop, Faith sighed, deciding she might as well just get this over with since the man seemed intent on prying into her personal life.

"She's dead." Her words hung in the air for a moment, echoing around them in the quiet confines of the car.

"I'm so very sorry." He gave her hand a comforting squeeze. "It is very difficult to lose someone you love, Faith. Very difficult." The thought of Jalila flashed through his memory, but only for the briefest moment. "And your father?"

"My father?" Her eyes flashed and her voice went cold. "My father killed my mother." She said it matter-of-factly, then made the mistake of looking at Ali and saw the horror on his face.

"Not literally," she clarified. "With his actions.

But regardless of how he did it, it still had the same results.''

She shrugged, trying to dismiss the feelings of anger and bitterness that rose when she thought of her father.

"I really don't know where my father is," she admitted, turning to face Ali, tucking her legs under her on the seat and sighing. "My father never had much interest in me. He abandoned my mother and me when I was fourteen."

"I see." Ali continued to hold her hand, in comfort, in empathy, not liking the unadulterated sadness echoing in her voice.

He wasn't going to ask the details, she knew, because he was far too polite, far too cultured. But Faith had gone this far, she might as well go the distance. It had been so long since she'd allowed herself to talk about this with anyone, to think about it, she found the memories suddenly flooding back.

"My father was handsome, charming and a conman. He couldn't hold a decent job, couldn't stay faithful and couldn't tell the truth to save his life, but my mother was totally and completely devoted to and dependent on him." Her voice had turned bitter and Faith blew out a breath, still unable to understand or fathom her mother's blind devotion.

She shook her head. "My mother believed him, no matter what outrageous, ridiculous lies he told her. No matter what cruel things he did. She still believed him and believed *in* him." Her voice had gone very soft. Ali was still holding her hand, and she found herself clinging to him, to his comforting warmth, perhaps because she'd had so little comfort in her life.

"But you did not?"

She shook her head, a faint hint of a smile on her lips. "Nope. Even as a kid I wasn't an idiot. I'd heard every lie he'd ever told, knew he could charm birds out of the trees. I recognized at a young age exactly what he was. Perhaps that's why he never had much use for me."

Ali could see her at that age. Serious, responsible, just as she was now. And not a person to suffer fools.

He felt a sharp stab of pride and admiration for her.

But he also felt a wealth of sadness for her. To learn such realities at such a tender age must have been very difficult.

Faith stared off into the distance, absently watching the beautiful coastline fly by, remembering that painful time.

"Even as a child, I guess I always felt responsible for my mother," she said quietly. "She was just so…emotionally fragile, and so dependent on my father. She believed he was the prince charming all the fairy tales had promised." She shook her head. "I guess I always felt as if it was my job to prevent her from getting hurt." She sighed heavily. "I would have had an easier time stopping the sun from rising." She smiled sadly. "My mother was like…like an innocent child—always hopeful, always believing that everything would turn out all right. She believed in the fairy tale, the happily-ever-after." Inhaling a deep breath, Faith tried to push back the overwhelming sense of sadness that engulfed her whenever she thought of her mother. "But there was no happily-ever-after, at least not for my mom."

"What happened?" Ali asked, his voice soothing.

Reaching for her soda, Faith took a long sip, needing to soothe her dry, aching throat.

"When I was about fourteen, after another one of my father's very public affairs—affairs he didn't bother to hide from me, my mother or anyone else—he finally returned home, apologized and begged my mother to take him back, promising it would never happen again, that he loved her—us—and had big plans." Faith's laugh was bitter and she shook her head. "She believed him."

"But you did not." It wasn't a question, merely a statement.

"A leopard doesn't change his spots."

"What happened?" he prompted.

"He had my mother pack up the house, and all our belongings, said he had some big fancy job in New York. That he'd rented a house for us, with a big backyard, and that we were finally going to live the good life, be a real family."

Faith's eyes burned with unshed tears so she closed her eyes for a moment, trying to gather her composure.

Wisely, Ali said nothing, merely held her hand in his and waited until she was ready to continue.

"I remember..." She smiled. "I remember how excited I was at the time. I secretly hoped that this time was different. He wouldn't lie to us again, not about something so important. I desperately wanted that house with the big backyard, and a real family like all the other kids had. A father who didn't lie or run around with other women, who came home after work and did nothing but sit in a chair and watch ball games, or took me out for ice cream once in a while.

Just that once, I allowed myself to...hope." She rolled her shoulders, trying to ease the tension. "He said he had to go to New York to finalize the deal, but he'd be back in less than a week to get us." Her voice had dropped to a choked whisper, causing Ali to tighten his hand on hers.

"There was no job?" Ali asked softly, wishing horsewhipping was still legal. He would personally take a whip to her father for his cruel behavior.

"Not only was there no job, there was no house, either. It had all been lies, nothing but lies." She pressed her fingers to her eyes for a minute, took a deep breath then continued. "I was devastated and so ashamed. I *knew* better. I knew I shouldn't have hoped or believed him. I felt stupid and humiliated, and as gullible as my mother." She blew out a long, deep breath. "I felt old, weary and just a bit too wise for my age."

Looking at her, he could still see the devastated fourteen-year-old child, her dreams shattered, her hopes dashed, her heart broken. It made his own heart ache in a way it had not in many years.

"My mother had dutifully packed up all of our belongings. The boxes were stacked very neatly in a row in the living room just waiting to be carted out. Then we waited. Every day I'd come home from school and my mother would just be sitting by the front window, staring out, waiting for him like a little kid waiting patiently for Santa Claus." She turned to Ali and he could see the sparkle of tears in her eyes.

"He never came back?"

"No." Her voice was whisper-soft. "We never heard from him again. My mother never got over it.

She never stopped staring out that window, never stopped waiting for him." Faith wiped at the tears that filled her eyes, annoyed that this could still hurt after so many years. "Day by day I watched the life ebb out of my mother bit by bit, and nothing I did seemed to help or stop it. I didn't know how to make it better, how to make her better." Her voice caught, and she had to swallow hard.

"I am sorry, Faith. So very sorry." The sadness, the hopelessness in her voice tore at his heart, and he brought her hand to his lips and held it there.

She had only been fourteen, just past childhood, but not yet an adult. A time when life should have been filled with friends, parties, boys and wonderful carefree memories.

He thought of his own wondrous childhood. He'd spent three months of his fourteenth year cruising the Mediterranean with his parents on the royal family yacht, never once giving a thought to anything more serious than what to order for lunch, or what color trunks to wear for his afternoon swim.

Knowing how different their lives had been, realizing how blessed he'd been to have the kind of life and parents he had humbled him and made him enormously grateful.

He kissed her hand, wanting to give comfort as well as receive it.

"What could you do, Faith? I mean, you were a mere child."

She took a moment to gather her thoughts, her composure.

"I had to do something, so I did the only thing I knew how to do. I grew up. Fast." She shrugged her shoulders restlessly. "I had no choice. I had to take care of my mother because after a while, it became clear something in her had finally snapped."

For the first time, her throat clogged. She hadn't cried about her mother in years. Hadn't cried or thought of the terror she felt, knowing that day by day her mother was slipping further and further away from her, into her own little world where no one could reach her.

Not even her daughter.

She'd been terrified, alone, not knowing what to do, whom to turn to. Faith shivered now as the memories surfaced. Sometimes when she closed her eyes at night she could still see her mother, sitting, waiting, with her nose pressed against that window.

"Within two months, the bank foreclosed on the house because the mortgage hadn't been paid."

"You lost your home?" he asked, horrified.

She nodded. "Once we lost the house, we had nowhere to go. I was in my freshman year of high school and my baby-sitting jobs were barely enough to keep food on the table, let alone pay a mortgage."

She sounded so guilty, Ali's anger at her father stirred again. "You should not have had to even deal with such responsibilities at that age, Faith."

"Yeah, well, what I should have had and what I had were two very different things."

"What happened after you lost your house? Where did you go?"

"With the help of the county, I was able to get my mother into a medical facility. She'd suffered a complete breakdown." Faith glanced down and absently pleated the crease in her slacks. "I cried for days and days after I had to leave her there. I knew she'd be scared, terrified.'' Pressing a hand to her mouth, she refused to let the tears fall. ''Hell, I cried for days because *I* was scared and terrified.'' She pushed a tumble of curls off her face, then took a slow, deep breath.

''I went to see her almost every day, and every day when I arrived, I'd find her sitting at the window, even in the institution, waiting, certain my father was coming for her. She sat in that window waiting every single day until the day she died.'' Faith glanced at Ali. ''He never came back.''

''Oh, Faith.'' There were no words that could ease the sorrow and pain that she had endured, nothing that would ease or erase the awful memories that had etched a place in her heart. If there was, he would find it.

''What happened to you after your mother…passed away?''

''Right after she was institutionalized, the county social workers sent me to live at the Hopechest Ranch. After her death, I had nowhere else to go so I lived there until I finished high school. When I turned eighteen, I left for college, working my way through fixing computers. I'd become interested in them while I was living at the ranch.'' She shrugged. ''After college, I applied for a Small Business Administration loan and opened my own computer consulting firm. The rest is history.''

''Faith, I am so very, very sorry.''

''Don't be. What happened is in the past, but I did learn a valuable lesson from it.''

''What lesson?'' he asked with a frown.

"I learned that I'd never, ever make the mistakes my mother made, certainly not about a man. Not *any* man," she added firmly, looking at him. "I'd never trust or believe a man I knew to be a womanizer or a liar. I'd never trust or believe a man who cared so little for others' feelings that he'd deceive people he loved."

Guilt washed over Ali like a tidal wave. From her tone, he wasn't certain if she was talking about her father or *him*.

"Faith, you cannot possibly believe for a minute that I am anything like your father." The thought horrified him as nothing in his life ever had before. "Surely you cannot believe that I would—"

"Would what, Ali?" she asked softly. "Deliberately lie to someone you love? Deliberately deceive them?"

Disheartened, he stared at her for a long moment, realizing what she said was true, in the strictest sense, but both times his lies, his deceptions had been to spare a loved one's feelings—Maureen Jourdan's and his parents'—not to hurt them. He could not even conceive of such an action.

But clearly, Faith did not see or want to see the distinction. And he knew he had no defense against her words.

But now, now, he finally understood why she reacted so strongly each time she believed him to be deceiving someone he loved.

But how on earth would he ever get her to see the man he truly was?

Twelve

Palm Springs

"**Y**our home is magnificent," Faith said in amazement, as Tibi showed her around the El-Etra estate.

Set on five secluded acres, the home was a two-story stone and brick Tudor surrounded by lush gardens, fountains and enormous gardens.

A discreet guarded gate prevented prying eyes or unwelcome visitors from exploring the enormous estate in one of the most exclusive enclaves in Palm Springs.

Linking her arm through Faith's, Tibi smiled as she led her around the back gardens, toward the patio that overlooked the sparkling pool where Omar and Ali were having a before-dinner drink.

"Thank you, Faith dear. Although our main home

is in Kuwait, we wanted to have something here in the States so that we would have an excuse to visit our son.'' With a laugh, Tibi patted Faith's arm. ''When you have children of your own you will understand that no matter how old they get, they are still your children and you worry about them.''

''So did you enjoy your tour?'' Omar asked, getting up to greet them.

Faith smiled. ''Yes, very much. Your home is lovely.''

Omar took her hand, and led her to one of the plush ivory garden chairs. ''You are to consider it your home now as well, dear.''

''Would you like something cold to drink, Faith?'' Tibi took the chair next to her husband. ''Or would you prefer to rest before our guests arrive?''

''Guests?'' Faith shot a nervous glance at Ali, who had been surprisingly quiet since they'd arrived. He shrugged his shoulders, clearly clueless about this turn of events.

Tibi smiled. ''Yes, I hope you don't mind. But we've invited a few old friends over for dinner. We are so very happy that Ali has finally found happiness, we wanted to have a chance to show you off, so to speak.'' Tibi reached for Faith's hand, a slight frown on her elegant face. ''I hope you don't mind, dear. It's just friends, and nothing fancy. We're actually going to have a simple barbecue.'' She glanced at her watch. ''In fact, the caterers should be arriving shortly to set everything up.''

A *few* old friends? Simple barbecue? With caterers? Feeling a bit overwhelmed, but determined to hide it,

Faith forced a smile she didn't feel, grateful once again that she'd spent the morning shopping.

"No, of course I don't mind." She smiled to hide her nervousness. "I'd be honored to meet your friends."

Tibi glanced at her husband. "We could not let the occasion of our son's engagement pass without having a bit of a celebration." She looked so joyous, Faith didn't have the heart to put a damper on her mood. But the thought of being the center of attention at a dinner was enough to make her feel faint.

"Well, as long as there will be guests for dinner, perhaps I should go upstairs and rest for a bit." Faith stood up, needing some time alone.

"Ali, show Faith to her room, sweetheart. I put her in the guest room in the west wing, in the room adjacent to yours."

Ali drained his glass of mineral water, then stood up. "I'll be happy to, Mom." Dutifully, he took Faith's hand, gently tugging her close. "I think I'll rest for a while, too. I'm tired from the drive, and I had a long night last night."

"You're working too hard," Tibi said, leaning back in her chair to beam at the happy couple. "Faith, once you are married, you should insist he come home at a decent hour and have dinner with you. Being a workaholic is fine when you're a single man, but now that you will have a family, Ali, your priorities need to change."

"Do not lecture, dear," Omar said with affection, reaching out to stroke his wife's cheek. "Let the children be. They will find their own way, as we once did."

"You are right, dear," Tibi said with a laugh. "Go now, go rest before dinner. I'll call you in plenty of time to freshen up and change."

"Good grief, this room is big enough to house a football team," Faith said as Ali led her into the beautiful two-room suite that would be her home for the weekend. Knowing his room was right next door—a quick glance told her there was a connecting door—only added to her nerves.

"I hope you will be comfortable here," Ali said as he went to the double French patio doors and opened them wide, letting in the fresh afternoon air.

"Comfortable?" Faith did a slow pirouette, trying to take everything in. "I could probably hide out in here and it would take months for anyone to find me."

The room, done in beautiful shades of pink and lime-green, was a vision of elegance. The huge canopy four-poster bed looked to be a genuine antique, as did all the other exquisite pieces of furniture.

The carpeting was a plush lime, while the walls were papered in a delicate pink-and-lime silk stripe. A pink-and-green overstuffed satin chaise longue sat at a comfortable angle to the patio doors, allowing one to sit and merely observe the beautiful gardens below.

A mahogany English writing desk was snuggled into one corner. It, too, had a matching pink-and-green striped chair.

Double doors leading to a sumptuous bath were open, allowing Faith to see the huge, sunken marble tub large enough for ten.

Around the room were various sized vases filled with beautiful pink roses, no doubt from Tibi's magnificent gardens.

"I need to unpack." Nervous tremors were shaking her knees and causing her stomach to flip-flop. She wished he'd leave so she could fall apart quietly. She didn't want him to know his mother's announcement had terrified her.

"It's been done for you," he said with a quiet nod toward the walk-in closet.

"Oh." She wasn't accustomed to having servants do things for her and she wasn't certain she was comfortable with it. But when in Rome, she thought, turning to Ali to find him watching her curiously, quietly.

"What?" she asked, trying not to fidget under his dark, intense gaze.

"You are upset, Faith."

"Upset? Me?' She tried to laugh, but her throat had gone dry and it came out a croak. "Why would I be upset?"

He merely watched her, gauging her mood. "You are nervous about tonight, and the guests." It wasn't a question, but a statement, and she cursed the fact that she was so transparent.

She twisted her damp hands together. "Ali..." She flushed. "I'm not very good with people," she admitted miserably. "I don't have much experience socializing."

To see strong, independent Faith struggling with nerves over a little party touched him beyond measure. She had bravely gone through so much at such a young age, that the thought that something like a small social gathering could fluster her tugged at his heart.

She had done so many things without anyone to help her, to protect her, but this, he silently vowed, she would not go through alone or unprotected.

He would not allow anything to fluster her or frighten her, not while he was around.

He'd gotten to know and judge her moods very well and could see the quiet desperation clawing through her. It made his heart ache because she was trying so hard to be strong, and brave.

For him, he realized. She'd done this for him. And his parents.

"Do not worry," he said softly, going to her to take her hands in his and giving them a reassuring squeeze. He wanted to draw her into his arms, to wrap them tightly around her, to hold her, shield her so that she never feared anything ever again.

"It will only be my parents' friends," he said gently, hoping to soothe some of her nerves.

"Yes, but—" She had to swallow. She was nervous enough without having him right in front of her, touching her. Her thoughts scattered like leaves in a fall wind. Why she bothered to think and talk when he was so close, when he was touching her, was a mystery. She forced herself to concentrate. "I really am not very good at small talk or chitchat." She shrugged, glancing past him so she wouldn't have to lose herself in those magnificent eyes of his. "People really do make me nervous. I've always been far more comfortable with machines."

"So you've told me." He wondered if she knew how utterly irresistible she looked at this moment?

"And what am I going to say to these people?" Flustered, her gaze searched his. "I mean they're going to want to know all about me, and there's not much to tell." She frowned. "I don't like talking about my personal life, what there is of it, and then of course, they're going to want to know all about us, about the engagement, the wedding. Good Lord—" She broke off, getting more unsettled by the minute. "Ali, I don't have any answers for them."

And the thought terrified her. Just the thought of being put on the spot, having to deal with questions she had no answers for, made her nearly cringe.

This little deception of theirs was getting more complicated by the minute.

She tilted her head back to look at him, and then realized it was a mistake. His face, that glorious mouth, was barely inches from hers. Her memory replayed the impact that mouth had on her and her body reacted immediately, filling her with an intense type of longing she wasn't quite sure what to do about.

She swallowed, feeling her own mouth go dry.

"Faith, please, do not worry." Unable to watch her discomfort, he drew her into the comforting circle of his arms. "Do not worry. I will take care of everything." Gently, he rubbed his hands up and down her back. "I promise I will not leave your side." He rested his head atop her hair. She fit perfectly, he thought, allowing himself the pleasure of concentrating solely on the feel of her against him. The way she smelled, that wonderful, sweet, feminine scent that always seemed to linger in his senses. The soft curves of her breasts, her hips. The way those long legs of hers brushed against his.

He drew back to look at her. "I will be with you every moment, stuck to you like a sticky piece of gum to the bottom of a shoe."

"Well now, there's an image," she said with a smile, realizing he was deliberately trying to lighten the mood.

"We are in this together, Faith."

Together. The word reverberated around in her mind.

Together.

With Ali.

But just for this weekend, she reminded herself sternly. And only for pretend.

"I just don't want to do anything to embarrass your parents. I—" She frowned, then thought better of what she was going to say, instead, merely sliding her arms around his waist and ordering all the tension to leave her body.

With a sigh, Faith allowed herself to relax against him, to let his warmth and words comfort her. Wearily, she laid her head on his shoulder, realizing how good it felt, how comfortable it seemed, how right it was.

Stunned by her confession, he drew back, looked deep into her eyes, his heart aching with a burgeoning emotion he refused to name or identify.

"Is that what this is about?" he asked softly, searching her face. "You are concerned about perhaps embarrassing my parents?" How could she know that nothing could have touched his heart more?

Looking at him, she nodded miserably, unable to tell him how important this was to her. She knew she was not the type of woman *he* could love, knew it and was trying to accept it, but clearly, his parents didn't feel the same way.

And they had been so kind to her, so totally accepting and loving, she wouldn't hurt them for the world.

"Oh Faith, how you move me." With a sigh, he pressed a kiss to her hair, her brow, her cheek, letting his mouth linger, savoring the sweetness of her. "You are the most incredible woman I have ever known." He kept sliding his mouth over her skin, letting his lips soothe and arouse. "You are so genuine, so real, so totally unaffected, you make my heart sing in a way I'd forgotten it could."

"Ali." His words made her own wary, scarred heart soften, hope. "Oh, Ali." She forgot all the warnings she'd reiterated a hundred times to herself since she'd agreed to spend the weekend with him, forgot everything but the man in her arms. Tilting her head, she raised her mouth for his. "Kiss me."

He did. It was neither gentle nor soothing, but hot, demanding, passionate. His arms tightened around her as his body responded to her closeness, to her softness, to his need for her—only her.

The first touch of his tongue on her lips and in her mouth had her whimpering softly, clinging to the back of his shirt, arching against him, wanting him to close the distance between them and become part of her.

She opened her mouth to him, greedy now for the touch and feel of him, giving back all she got. Her body trembled when his hands slid to her waist, then to her buttocks, to cup and caress, bringing her closer against his growing, aching hardness.

It was his turn to groan, a soft whisper of need that only fueled her own desire.

Need, raw and ripe, spiraled through her, making her body ache and moisten. Nearly mindless with desire, she ground herself against him, wanting to cool the ache of fire his touch had aroused.

"I want you," he murmured softly, sliding his mouth from hers to her neck, nipping gently at the tender skin there, before sliding down to suckle her breast right through the jacket of her silk pantsuit.

"Yes," Faith gasped as she threaded her fingers through his hair, holding his head and arching against him as he sucked her breast. Wanting to feel flesh to flesh, he slid his hand under the top, till finally he tugged it off and dropped it to the floor. She was bare beneath the jacket, her skin a beautiful shade of ivory, her breasts small, perfect, tipped with dark nipples.

"Faith." His breath withered out of him. "You are so beautiful." He lifted her in his arms and carried her toward the bed, bending his head to suckle her ripe, aching breasts as he lay her on the bed and followed her down.

With a moan, she tore at his shirt, lifting it out of his pants and tugging it open until the buttons went flying around the room like a hail of snow. She wanted to touch flesh, to feel his skin, warm and bare beneath her hands.

His mouth drove her higher and higher until her hips were arching and she was clinging to him, moaning softly, dying with need.

Half-mad with a desire to possess her, Ali tried to absorb every sensation. He wanted to see her, all of her, to feel that beautiful, pliant body respond to him, and only him.

"Faith." He dragged the silk pants that covered her from him down her legs, nearly ripping them in his madness.

It was as if a demon had possessed him. The need for her was so powerful, tugging him into a deep abyss of emotions he had never known existed. He wanted to brand her as his, so that no other man would ever know the joy of possessing her.

"You are so beautiful," he murmured, knowing in that moment, that no other woman could compare to her, not for him.

There was no fear of his frenzied, almost frantic desire, only a response that left him breathless, hot, hard and wanting only to satisfy this craving she had created in him.

A pulse thrummed hotly, incessantly between her legs, and she arched to help him skim her panties off her hips. She almost cried out when she felt his hand slide the scrap of silk down her legs, then merely whimpered at the fire he started, burning up his path until finally the fire settled into a white-hot pulse between her thighs.

Buffeted by myriad sensations, Faith let her hands frantically run over his bare back, wanting to absorb him into her. Mindless, she let her hands glide over his bare skin, savoring his touch, the feel of him.

Her nails dug in when he began to kiss his way down her body.

A moan of surprise, delight and desire ripped from her, and she clutched his hair when she felt the warmth of his lips glide over her thigh, moving slowly upward, causing her to arch.

At the first touch of his tongue between her legs, she cried out, closing her eyes and driving her hips against the intense pleasure he was giving her.

"Ali." She could barely say his name, she was so mindless to everything but the pleasure he was giving her, as he kissed her more intimately than anyone had ever done before.

Delirious and nearly desperate as he drove her higher, then higher still, her body quaked and she nearly screamed as his talented, clever mouth drove her over the edge in a haze of ecstasy so intense she was certain her heart would pound right out of her chest.

He didn't give her a chance to come down. He made his way up her body, up her belly, licking softly, nipping, then kissing where his teeth had gently nipped, moving upward to warm and excite her skin with his touch.

She reached for him, wanting him inside of her. He paused only long enough to shed his slacks, and then he was covering her with that magnificent male body, warm, strong, hard.

Gently, he kissed her eyes, then moved to her mouth, teasing her lips with his until she wrapped her arms around him, holding him closer, tighter.

"Ali, please?" she whispered in a pliant, husky plea. She couldn't wait anymore. When he rose above her, then slowly, carefully entered her, his eyes never leaving hers, her own eyes closed as wave after wave of feeling assaulted her.

Her breathing was shallow, harsh, as she moved

with him, arching against him, feeling him fill her. When he moved faster, she lifted her legs higher and wrapped them tighter around him, wanting to take him deeper. When she did, she heard his soft moan and saw his eyes darken.

The second peak of pleasure caught her by surprise, stealing her breath with the power and intensity of it. She cried out his name and clung to him, as he soared over the edge, taking her heart with him.

Something was brushing against her face. Her eyes fluttered open and she saw Ali smile down at her, brushing a tangle of hair off her face.

"You dozed for a few moments," he said softly, bending to kiss her.

Her mouth curved in a soft, slow smile. "Apparently." She was naked, relaxed and pressed intimately against him. She laid a hand to his cheek, overwhelmed by her feelings for him, for the experience they'd just shared. "You wore me out."

He laughed, bending to kiss her again. "And I have only just started," he said softly, deepening the kiss until she was moaning and arching against him. She wrapped her arms around him, enjoying the warmth of him. He groaned in regret, then pulled away. "Unfortunately, we cannot continue or we shall no doubt be late for dinner."

"Dinner." She scowled. "I almost forgot." Nerves started again, and she wanted to cling to him, to just stay right where she was.

Sensing her distress, he kissed her forehead. "Do not worry, Faith dear." He picked up her hand to kiss that as well. "Remember, I will be stuck to you—"

"Like sticky gum to a shoe," she finished with a nod. "I remember."

He smiled. "I have a present for you," he said softly, laughing when her eyes narrowed suspiciously. "You are suspicious again."

She sighed, feeling totally comfortable with him in spite of her nakedness. "Another present?" She shook her head. "I wish you'd stop buying me presents."

"Ahh, but you liked the last one," he said, sitting up and taking her with him.

"That's only because I'm a sucker for candy, soda and chips."

"I think you will like this present a bit better." Oblivious to his nakedness, he slid from the bed and crossed to the doors that connected their rooms. Faith watched him, letting her gaze soak up his magnificent body. As males went, she had to admit he was one incredible specimen.

When he returned, he handed her a small black velvet box. She eyed it warily. "What is this?"

"You won't know until you open it, now will you?" He touched her cheek. "Open it."

She did, and gasped. "Good Lord, what on earth is this?"

He laughed. "It is a ring, Faith. Your engagement ring."

"No," she said with a shake of her head. "This is a miniature ice skating rink." The diamond glinted and sparkled like a wondrous star. "Exactly how...how..." She was afraid to ask. "How big is this?"

His brows drew together thoughtfully. "I believe almost ten carats."

She almost dropped it. "I can't accept this." She pushed the box toward him with nervous fingers.

He stared at her. "And why not?"

"Good Lord, Ali, what if I lose it?" The mere thought had her stomach hitching.

He shrugged. "Then we will simply replace it."

"Replace it," she repeated, unable to take her eyes off the magnificent ring. It was a slender platinum band, with one single spectacular diamond set in the middle, surrounded by a slender braided band of platinum.

He took the ring out of the box and reached for her hand. "You are supposed to be my betrothed." He slid it on her finger, then smiled in approval. It fit perfectly as he knew it would. "I certainly cannot give you a cigar band for an engagement ring."

"Well, I'd probably feel more comfortable." She couldn't stop staring at the ring, her heart aching because she knew this was pretend…this was all pretend.

He kissed her forehead, then drew her close. Her naked breasts pressed against his bare chest and he groaned, wanting her all over again. "It is a pity, but we must get ready." He ran his hands up and down her bare back. "Or else my mother will no doubt be up here wanting to know what's taking us so long."

"Your mother?" She scrambled for the sheet to cover herself. "Good Lord, your mother can't see me like this."

He laughed, then pressed another kiss to her brow before standing. "We are engaged, Faith. Trust me, my mother would not be alarmed to find that we have made love. It is merely a way to show and share our love. Now I'll go to my own room and prepare for the evening." If he didn't leave now, he was afraid he might not. "You will be all right?" he asked with some concern.

"Fine. Just fine." Dragging her gaze from the ring, she lifted it to his, then smiled at his concern. "I'll be fine, Ali, really." She waved him away with her hand. "Now scoot so I can get showered and dressed."

True to his word, Ali never left her side all evening. Holding her hand, he introduced her to friends, answered all the questions, filled her dinner plate, tended to her drink, and was the ultimate attentive fiancé. By mid-evening, Faith's nerves had fled and she was actually enjoying herself. Tibi and Omar's friends were pleasant and pleased that Ali had finally decided to settle down. They were nothing but kind to her.

His parents had treated her as one of the family, proudly introducing her to everyone, making it clear that they couldn't be more pleased with their son's choice.

Now, as the evening wound down, Faith found herself feeling exhausted, enormously grateful most of the guests had gone and just a bit guilty.

Sipping a glass of wine, she slipped away from Ali and walked out onto the patio where they'd had drinks that afternoon.

The night was a perfect pitch black with stars glistening as brightly as the diamond on her finger. It had been a perfect evening, she realized sadly. Too perfect.

Guilt over their deception, and the fear that she would not be able to hide her true feelings for Ali much longer had Faith gnawing her lip in worry.

What had started out as a simple favor had turned into something far more complex. She glanced up at the stars and felt tears sting her eyes.

There was no denying how she felt about Ali. She couldn't deny what was in her heart, and now, knowing they'd made love, knowing just how wonderful they were together, had only made it worse.

He could never love her, he'd admitted it.

She had to accept it, but how could she accept it while she was playing the role of the loving fiancée?

Faith knew she couldn't. She couldn't bear to go on with this, couldn't bear to see the joy and relief in his parents' eyes, knowing it was going to break their hearts when they learned the truth. She couldn't bear to know that he could never love her as she loved him. Couldn't bear the thought that she had fallen hopelessly, heedlessly in love with him.

Realizing she couldn't go through with this any longer, Faith turned from the patio and, with a heavy heart, headed inside. She had to put an end to this deception for all their sakes.

The only question was how.

Thirteen

—

She was gone.

Ali awoke to an empty bed. He had spent the night in Faith's room. They had made love again and again, and then somewhere near dawn they'd fallen asleep in each other's arms.

But now the bed beside him was empty. Rubbing his eyes, he glanced around, noted her suitcase, which had been sitting on the floor in the now-open closet door was gone, as were all her clothes.

Panic had him climbing out of bed. "Faith?" He searched her suite, but she was gone and every trace that she had ever been there was gone as well. "Faith?" There was panic in his voice, in his heart. He went to his own room, pulled on a pair of jeans and a shirt, and headed downstairs, racing barefoot through the house. There was still no trace of Faith, and his panic increased.

"Mom?"

"In the kitchen." She was pouring herself a cup of coffee, while his father sat, reading the morning paper.

"Where's Faith?" he asked, glancing around.

"She's gone, Ali," his mother said quietly.

"Gone?" He scowled. "Gone where?"

"She told us the truth, Ali," his mother said softly, glancing at him. "Everything."

Guilt hit him with the force of an anvil and he sank down on a chair. "Mom, I'm sorry, I didn't mean to—"

Feeling sorry for him because he looked so utterly miserable, she patted his shoulder.

"I understand, son. You were concerned about our welfare." She cast a quick glance at Omar, who continued to read his paper. "I understand you did what you did out of love. Perhaps I don't agree with it, but I do understand." She poured him a cup of coffee, then handed it to him. "However, I cannot so easily understand how you could hurt Faith."

"Hurt Faith?" The coffee was so hot it almost scalded his tongue. "I never meant to hurt her," he grumbled, dragging a hand through his hair.

"She loves you," his mother said softly, causing him to glance up at her sharply.

"No, Mom." His laugh was soft and bitter. "On this you are wrong. She hates me," he said glumly, realizing it was true. "She thinks that I'm immoral and a liar."

Tibi nodded. "I understand the liar part. Ali, you have had better days," his mother admitted with a smile. "But you're wrong if you do not believe she loves you." She touched his hair. "Son, your father and I knew all along that you and Faith were not truly engaged."

"What?" Stunned, he merely stared at his mother.

She nodded. "We are not fools, son. But when we met Faith, we realized how perfect she was for you, how right. I knew you were not telling me the truth about the engagement—a mother always does." She smiled. "But I could see how much you loved her. I arranged this weekend as a means to get you to realize your feelings for Faith."

"Mom." Ali shook his head. "I will never fall in love again."

Tibi sighed. "Ali, I know how devastated you were when you lost Jalila, but that was a very long time ago, and you were just a boy. You are a man now, and should not allow the pain of the past to deny you happiness in the future."

"Mom, love is not necessary for a happy life or a happy marriage." He glanced up at her. "Look at you and Father."

Tibi's elegant brow arched upward. "Excuse me?" She stared at her only son in surprise. "What does our marriage have to do with this?"

Ali shrugged. "You and Father have not shared love. Oh, you have shared so many other wonderful things together, been true partners, but you are proof that love is not necessary to make a marriage work."

"I see," she said with a nod. "Omar?"

"Yes, dear." He continued to read his paper, turning a page. He had known his wife for too many years to not know when there was a fire simmering within her, and he had no wish to willingly step into the cinders.

"Did you perhaps drop our only son on his head when he was a child, and neglected to mention it to me?"

"No, dear."

She turned to Ali. "Then there is no excuse for such stupidity, my son. If you believe that your father and I have no love between us, then you are a blind fool. While it is true our marriage was arranged, your father and I have shared a deep and abiding love almost from the moment we met."

Ali merely stared at his mother in surprise. "You and Father...love each other?"

Annoyed, Tibi gave Ali a gentle smack to the back of his head. "You are too wise a man to be so blind, Ali. How could you not know how deeply your father and I love each other and you?" Feeling sorry for him, she sat down in the chair next to him and laid a hand on his arm. "You are in love with Faith, are you not?"

"No." He shook his head, unwilling to admit what his heart already acknowledged.

Her eyes widened. "Do not lie to yourself, Ali. A man who cannot admit the truth to himself is merely a fool."

Ali swallowed a sip of his coffee, too miserable for words.

"Do you love her, son?" Tibi persisted, and Ali blew out a breath, feeling as if he was standing on a shaky edge of a cliff.

"Yes." He shook his head, unable to believe that the feelings he'd tried so hard to avoid had snuck up on him, catching him unaware. "Yes, I love her," he admitted glumly. "And I...I do not know what to do now."

Miserable, he realized he had done the unthinkable, the unforgivable—he'd fallen hopelessly in love with Faith—and knew she would never, ever forgive him, or believe that he was not the immoral man she believed him to be.

Tibi laughed, patting his hand. "You are resourceful and headstrong, son, as well as bright, on occasion," she said with a mother's love. "I trust you will figure out what it is you should do." Tibi reached in her robe pocket and laid the black velvet box on the table between them. "I think this belongs to Faith?" She glanced at the box, then at her son. "I think perhaps you should return it to her, and this time, make sure it stays where it belongs."

Nervous as a cat, Faith paced in front of the window, not knowing what to do with herself. It had been over a week since she'd fled Ali's parents' Palm Springs home, a week of ignoring his calls, his flowers, his e-mails. Heartsick, she couldn't give in, wouldn't give in. She loved him and deserved to be loved back.

He couldn't love her; he'd admitted it, and she refused to accept anything less in her life.

She didn't want to see him or talk to him, but today was their meeting with Abner Josslyn. Mr. Josslyn had called and asked if they could meet at her office since he was pressed for time and on his way to the airport. He wanted to get a look at her operation, he'd said, and then casually mentioned he wanted Ali at the meeting.

She couldn't refuse, not without looking totally unprofessional, something she wouldn't do, not for anyone. Especially now that her company was poised on the verge of major success, thanks to the bonus from the El-Etra contract.

So now she paced, waiting for them to arrive. She went to the window again, pressed her nose against it, waiting, watching for Ali. When she realized what she was doing, she felt the sting of tears in her eyes.

Just like her mother.

Sitting at a window, waiting, watching for a man who had lied to her, deceived her.

Swallowing the lump in her throat, Faith stood up, swiped at her eyes, then slipped her hands in the pocket of her pantsuit.

"Faith."

She whirled at the sound of his voice, stunned to see Ali standing in the doorway of her office. She'd never even heard the door open. Her eyes greedily drank him in and her heart ached even more.

"How did you get in?" She pressed a hand to her pounding heart. "How did you get past Martha?"

He smiled slowly, stepping into the room and shutting the door softly behind him. "I bribed her," he said simply, making Faith gape at him. He laughed, slowly crossing the room to her. "That was a joke, Faith." He wanted to haul her into his arms and kiss away the shadows and tears that he saw in her eyes, her face.

"It wouldn't surprise me if you resorted to bribes," she snapped, restless and annoyed. She began to prowl the room, afraid to stand still, afraid to let him get too close.

"Where is Mr. Josslyn?"

"He is not coming."

Her gaze shot to his and her temper simmered. "What do you mean he's not coming?"

Ali shrugged. "He canceled."

Disappointment now joined heartbreak. "Then what are you doing here?"

"I came to talk to you."

"Did it occur to you that I don't want to talk to you?" She kept moving, unable to stand still.

"Yes, Faith, it did, since you refused my calls, did not respond to my e-mails and basically have ignored me for over a week."

"And I intend to keep ignoring you."

"I was wrong, Faith."

That caused her to pause. She was standing with her back to the windows. "Wrong?" She never thought she'd ever hear him admit he was wrong about anything. "About what?" she asked suspiciously, making him laugh.

"About you. About me." He moved closer, pinning her between him and the windows so he could talk to her. "I was wrong about being able to love."

She frowned. "What do you mean 'being able to love.'" She shook her head and pressed a hand to her temple. "You made it very clear that you could never love a woman like me."

He moved closer, causing her to retreat until her back was pressed against the windowsill. "No, I did not say I could not love a woman like you, Faith," he said softly. "What I said was that I could not love." He sighed, desperately searching for the right words. "After Jalila died, I felt as if I had died as well. I had loved her very much, Faith, and knew that I could not go through that kind of emotional pain ever again." He smiled sadly. "I did not ever want to be vulnerable to a woman, to know that she could mean the world to me and I could lose her." He shook his head. "Such a thing would simply devastate me."

"Are you saying that you made a decision not to fall in love because you didn't ever want to get hurt?"

"Something like that," he admitted. No longer able to be so close to her without touching her, he stroked a finger down her cheek. "But that was before I met you, before you stormed into my office, stormed into my life and tossed it upside down."

Hope slowly began to bloom, but she cautiously tried to stem it. "What are you saying, Ali?" She caught his hand as he stroked her cheek, clinging to his warmth, loving his touch, loving him.

"I am saying, dear Faith, that I love you." His eyes closed and the enormous shackle that had manacled his heart for so long simply slid away, leaving him feeling free, hopeful and very happy. "I love you more than anything in this world. You are the world to me."

"Oh, Ali." The tears came now, but this time they were tears of joy.

"I do not ever want to make you cry again," he said, alarmed by her tears. Lifting his free hand, he wiped away the dampness from her cheek. "I want you to marry me, Faith, to live with me, to love me, to have my children—*our* children—to grow old with me, and stay with me, and…and walk beside me no matter how unsteady the ground.'' His gaze searched hers, his love visible in his eyes. ''Please believe me, Faith, that I am truly an honorable man, and will honor you all the days of our lives. Please say that you will marry me.''

''Oh, Ali.'' She flung herself in his arms, clinging to him, wrapping her arms tightly around his neck and holding on for dear life. ''I love you, too, with all my heart. And yes, yes, I will marry you.''

''Faith.'' Relief weakened his knees and he dragged her closer, feeling as if the world had once again righted itself. ''You are all I have ever wanted but never thought I could have. All that I have ever needed.'' He pressed kisses all over his face, framing it with his hands. ''I shall love you for an eternity, Faith Martin. And then some.''

''And I will love you for an eternity, Ali.'' She kissed him back, her heart soaring. ''And then some.''

Drawing back, he laughed. ''And now we shall go to my parents and tell them the news.'' He reached in his pocket and pulled out the small velvet box. ''I believe this belongs to you.''

With a sigh, Faith slipped her ring back on her finger. Where it belonged. Where it had always belonged.

''I will want a quick wedding, Faith. I do not want to wait any longer than necessary.''

She nodded in agreement as he guided her toward the door. ''Fine with me. Ali, where are we going?''

''To celebrate,'' he said with a smile. ''And to tell my parents. My mother will be so happy. She will finally get those redheaded grandchildren she has always wanted.''

"Let's get the wedding over before we start having grandchildren.'' Faith slid her hand in his as they walked together toward the elevators. "But then I'd like to start as soon as possible.''

The elevator doors opened and they stepped in. "Yes, Faith, as soon as possible. Oh, I almost forgot.'' He reached in his pocket and pulled out some papers, handing them to her.

"What is this?'' she asked suspiciously.

He laughed and kissed her nose. "It is a contract for you to update all of Abner Josslyn's systems. For all his companies,'' he specified, making her gape at him.

"All?''

He nodded. "All.'' He took the contract and slipped it back into his pocket and then drew her into his arms. "But it shall be a while, Faith, before you can do the Josslyn job.'' He kissed her deeply. "I have another contract for you to fulfill. A marriage contract. After that, anything else you want to do is fine.'' He kissed her again. "I love you, Faith.''

"And I love you.''

Still holding each other, they stepped out of the elevator and toward their new life, their future, together.

Look for the next book
in the Coltons' series
The Doctor Delivers
by Judy Christenberry
September 2001.

One

Liza could feel herself coming to depend on that sexy smile of the doctor's. And she was fascinated with the cleft in his chin. The urge to trace it with her finger was crazy, but it was there all the same.

She frowned, hoping to erase those thoughts and convince the doctor she was serious. "Must go."

Pushing the tray back, she tried to swing her legs off the bed, but he was blocking her way.

"I don't think so. Look, just give me twenty-four hours. We can—"

He broke off when she vigorously shook her head. And got dizzy.

"At least until the morning? I'll come to your room before you have breakfast. That will give you a night's rest, at least."

That plan sounded so tempting, she paused to give

it some consideration. But Emily— "Call hotel," she whispered. "Messages."

She received a level stare for her words. "*I'll* call for your messages," he said. "They wouldn't understand you anyway."

She knew none of the family would leave any inappropriate messages for strangers to hear, so she nodded and gave him the name of the hotel. Tensely she waited for him to report back to her after his brief conversation.

"Your mother called half an hour ago, shortly before she reached you here. And a few minutes ago a Mrs. Tremble called."

Liza frowned. She wasn't surprised by her mother's calls. But Mrs. Tremble? Somehow that name rang a bell but— Suddenly she sat straight up in bed and grabbed the doctor's wrist.

"What is it? Are you in pain?" he asked at once, leaning close to her.

Too close. She drew a deep breath and subsided against the pillow. "Mrs. Tremble's message?"

He looked at the pad he'd written the messages on. "She said she'd call back in twenty-four hours."

Relief and joy filled Liza. "Number?"

He shook his head.

She had no way to return the call, but she reminded herself that Emily was smart. She'd been clever enough to elude the man who'd tried to kill her. Smart enough to be alive.

Liza wanted to call Uncle Joe, but she couldn't. Emily wouldn't have used the name Mrs. Tremble if everything was okay. Mrs. Tremble was an old rag doll that had been Emily's constant companion during her youth. She'd known Liza would recognize the name.

"What's so important about that call?" Dr. Hathaway asked.

She beamed at him. "Important," she repeated, nodding.

"So you'll stay overnight?" he asked, watching her.

What could it hurt? She could get a good night's rest and feel better tomorrow. And her mother probably wouldn't call back at the hospital. She wouldn't have to deal with her until she felt better.

That thought alone eased the tightness in her stomach. But most of all, it was Emily's call that had her relaxing, letting her exhaustion creep in, sending her eyelids lower. Emily was still in trouble, but she was alive.

Liza tried to nod, to signify her agreement, but she wasn't sure she made it. Blessed sleep was taking over.

Nick watched his patient fade into sleep, curiosity rampant in his head. When he'd read the message, her electric response told him it was important. Now, as he watched the tension leave her body, he knew whatever had been bothering her was easing, allowing sleep to take charge.

She should show a good improvement in the morning if she slept twelve or fourteen hours, after taking in some nourishment. He'd join her for breakfast, make sure she ate. Then, if she insisted on leaving he couldn't legitimately hold her.

But he thought he'd drop by the hotel and personally question the operator who had taken the message from the mysterious Mrs. Tremble.

Liza Colton had caught his interest for a lot of different reasons, not least of which was the mystery that surrounded her.

He insisted it had nothing to do with her delicate beauty.